MAGGIE & OLIVER

or A Bone of One's Own

MAGGIE & OLIVER
or A Bone of One's Own

Valerie Hobbs

art by Jennifer Thermes

SCHOLASTIC INC.

ISBN 978-0-545-65548-4

12 11 10 9 8 7 6 5 4 3 2 1   14 15 16 17 18/0

Printed in the U.S.A.   40

First Scholastic printing, November 2013

Book designed by Véronique Lefèvre Sweet

For my grandson, Rafael
—V. H.

For Mom and Dad, with love
—J. T.

Heartfelt thanks to Reka Simonsen, who first saw the promise in Maggie and Oliver and got them on their way; to Noa Wheeler, who kept them alive; and to the brilliant Jennifer Thermes, who gave them faces, bodies, and a whole city to live in.

Contents

MAGGIE & OLIVER
or A Bone of One's Own

Bertie?

With his long, wet tongue, Oliver licked and licked Bertie's cheek. "Wake up," his tongue said. "It's time to get up!"

But Bertie would not wake up. Her eyelids did not flutter. She did not groan and swat her hand at him. She did not say, "Oh, Oliver, you pesky dog." She lay still beneath her quilt of many colors, and Oliver waited.

All night long, he had chased things in his dreams. Cats and trolley cars, snowflakes and tin cans. He had snored and snuffled, and his back legs ran and ran. Now he was hungry and wanted his breakfast.

He poked his nose into Bertie's hand and waited, his tail wagging, but she did not move.

He padded out to the kitchen to check his bowl again. It was still empty, licked clean from the night before. It was a very sad, empty bowl.

There was something quite wrong here, but Oliver did not know what it was. The house was quiet, strangely quiet. The squirrels in the attic were not chattering. Even the mice, awake before the sun, were quiet. Did they know something he didn't?

Only the clock on the mantelpiece wagged its golden tongue, *click-click*, back and forth, back and forth, as if it knew what was wrong but didn't much care.

The ice wagon came creaking up the road. Gerd, the iceman, was Oliver's friend. Gerd would know what to do. Down the steps Oliver ran, two by two by two, and out into the yard. Leaping against the fence, he howled for Gerd.

"Oliver—there, boy! What's the matter?" Gerd's brown face crumpled up like a washrag. He took Oliver's head in both his hands and rubbed him hard, the way Oliver liked to be rubbed. His brown eyes were tender. "What's all the fuss?" he said.

"Come and see!" Oliver said with his eyes. Some humans could read dog eyes, but Gerd was not one of them.

Gerd went to the back of the ice wagon just as he always did. With his tongs, he pierced a block of ice and hauled it through the gate. He went up the stairs, the ice block dripping. Oliver ran alongside, dodging the drops.

At the door, Gerd called out to Bertie, but she did not answer him. That is when Oliver let out the most awful howl.

"There, boy," said Gerd. "Calm down, now."

Gerd went into the kitchen. He opened the icebox and slid the block of ice inside. "Bertie?"

Oliver sprinted across the kitchen. He waited for Gerd at the bedroom door. When Gerd came, Oliver raced to Bertie's bed and pushed his nose into her cold hand once more. She did not move.

Gerd leaned over Bertie. He laid his hand against her cheek. He shook his head. "Oh, dear," he said.

Bertie's family came. Bertie was old, they said. It was her time to go. "Where?" asked Oliver with his eyes. "Where is Bertie going?"

But Bertie's family could not read dog eyes either. They ignored the brown dog. They fought over who would get the dining room table. Who would get the dishes and the mantelpiece clock. The clock clicked away as if it didn't care, but Oliver knew it did.

Oliver was hungry. Very sad and very hungry. He pushed his bowl all over the kitchen with his nose, but no one noticed.

The movers came and took everything away. There went Bertie's chair, there went her quilt. There went Oliver's dish! Oliver whined and yipped and ran in circles.

One of the movers patted Oliver's head. "Hey!" he called. "Who's taking the dog?"

No one did.

Now the house was empty and the fireplace cold. No rocking chair sat before it, no little black book for Bertie to read, no reading glasses to see the words with, no Bertie.

Oliver lay down where his rug used to be. He put his nose on his paws and tried to think. Without Bertie, who would brush his coat? Who would trim his whiskers? Who would fill his bowl?

Who would love him for being the special dog that he was?

Oliver knew what he must do. He must find Bertie. She would wake up, wherever she was, and look for him. She would swat at him and say, "Oh, Oliver, you pesky dog. Where have you been?"

Why hadn't he followed the wagon that took her away? By now, the trail would be cold.

An Owl, a Duchess, and Dust

"Get up this minute, you silly, lazy girl!"
Far down the row of narrow beds stood
Hannah, the head housekeeper. Her face was the
color of a ripe tomato, and her fists sat on her wide
hips like lumps of bread dough. "If Madame Dinglebush had found you before I did, out you would go.
You foolish, lazy girl."

Maggie hopped into her knickers, pulled on her
shift and gray dress. Tying her apron strings, she
started to tell Hannah about the owl. How she had
seen the big gray bird with bright red eyes that was
perched on a branch of the oak tree right outside the
window and—

Hannah had her by the arm and dragged her down the hall. "There"—she pointed—"under that bed. That's where you will find your owls. And lots of dust besides."

She shook a dust rag at Maggie's face. "You are living here only by the good graces of Madame, on whose doorstep you were found," she said. "Earn your keep, girl, or Madame will cast you out."

Maggie sneezed. With a sigh, she took the rag from Hannah's hand. She knew that Hannah was right. She was no longer a child. She was nearly eleven. She must perfect all the skills of keeping a fine house, or she would be out on the streets of Boston with nowhere to live.

Out on the streets. The cruel words trickled like ice water down her spine.

If only she could quiet her brain. What good was wondering about owls while the dust collected beneath Madame's bed? Maggie wriggled under the bedskirt. Sneezing, she began to dust.

It had been very late when she had heard the *hooo-hoo*ing of the owl. She had gotten up and hurried to the window of the room where she and all the other maids slept. High up in the branches of an oak tree was a huge dark shape against the moon.

"Woooo," called the owl, a deep trill.

Why was it calling? she wondered. Who was it calling? Was it seeking a mate? Did it live in this tree? Did owls live in the same tree all their lives? Was it a boy owl or a girl owl?

Maggie's head spun with so many questions, she could not sleep until the misty light of morning.

If only she didn't think so much, she would be a better housekeeper.

The Duchess of Landsaway was coming, and Madame was in a frenzy. Everything must be perfect for the evening meal—the long white tablecloth starched stiff as paper, every serving spoon polished as bright as the first evening star. When the duchess entered the grand salon, the maids were to stand in a straight line with their eyes forward. They were not to smile or curtsy. They were simply there for show. Madame would not have to brag about the number of maids she had. The duchess could see for herself and be very impressed.

It was the most important day of Madame's life. If all went well, the servants would be rewarded. Each would get a slice of pie, a small slice, perhaps with a drizzle of cream.

Maggie was excited. She had never seen a duchess. Would she look like Madame? Would her dress be grander? Did she live in a duchery? A dukery?

But Hannah was through with Maggie's questions. "I've told you all I know, child," she said. "Now get busy with your chores. And don't be late for the duchess's arrival!"

The Nose Knows

For once in his short life, Oliver was happy to be an ordinary mutt, with parts of many kinds of dogs all mixed together. The part of him that was bloodhound would help find Bertie. With one last sad look at the cozy house where he had been raised from a pup, Oliver headed into the wide open world.

Missy, the lady who liked him, and Blister, her cat who did not, sat side by side on their steps. "Where are you off to, Oliver?" said Missy. But Oliver had no time for chitchat. His mission had begun.

Bertie had taught him about streets, how to look both ways, when to cross and when to wait. She did not know that Oliver used his ears as much as his eyes, and his nose most of all. He always heard streetcars coming long before she saw them. He nudged her away from steaming piles of horse poop. He protected her from suspicious humans and stray cats, which, in Oliver's book, were smarter and meaner than dogs. Though he did not like the city much, he did not fear it. As Bertie often said, he was an intelligent beast with a good and kind heart.

The cobblestones were dirty and cold. But Oliver stuck his nose right down, the way you were supposed to when you were bloodhounding. He sniffed along, his good and kind heart brimming with hope. Was that her sitting alone on that porch? Alas, no. Was that her walking toward him with a bent head? No. The next street. She was bound to be on the next street, where she always went to buy food. He raced ahead.

"No dogs! No dogs!" cried the little stick man as Oliver raced around and around his food shop, sniffing the barrels of potatoes and flour and beans, and finding nothing. Not a whiff of Bertie anywhere.

On to the shop where Bertie bought their meat. More careful now, Oliver crept inside. He sniffed through the sawdust. But the sawdust made him sneeze and the big butcher came. "Out!" he thundered, and Oliver fled.

Growing ever more confused and downhearted, Oliver left the neighborhood he knew and crossed the big bridge into the place called Boston. This world was filled with a disharmony of smells, so many you could hardly tell one from another. Old men sleeping on benches, bottles spilled or broken, garbage wrapped in newspaper, dead animals crawling with flies.

He sniffed a wet shoe lying on its side in the gutter. It was not Bertie's. A lady smelling of soap passed. Not Bertie. Bertie smelled like applesauce and homemade bread. The world smelled mostly like horse poop. A cold wind moaned and, for a moment, stole the smells away. A trolley car clanged and clattered past. Filthy water and bits of trash ran in a river down the middle of the street.

As Oliver passed a tall brick building, a window on the third floor flew open. A pail filled with dirty water splattered and ran toward the gutter, narrowly missing Oliver's head.

Bloodhounding was dangerous work. How could you see what was aiming for your head if you had your nose always on the ground?

Then Oliver rounded a corner where the big bank stood, and the whole world changed. Now the air was filled with the tease of food, and he remembered that he'd had no breakfast. He threaded his way through women carrying shopping bags, not one of them Bertie, and loped past open stalls filled with apples, barrels of onions, potatoes, and turnips.

But such was not a dog's breakfast.

Inches above his head drifted the beguiling aroma of chicken grease. He followed it, growing hungrier with every step.

And there at last was breakfast, a dozen fat chickens roasting on a spit over a crackling fire. Oliver began to drool. His tail wagged for pure joy. He stood on his hind legs to get a better sniff.

"Out of here, you mangy cur!" A man, waving a broom, hurtled toward him. Oliver was too hungry to be proud. With little yapping sounds, he danced and begged for just a bite of breakfast.

But the man had angry, snapping eyes. He raised the broom over his head. Oliver bolted away as the broom came crashing down.

With nothing in his belly, Oliver got back on the trail. He began to think that finding food might be harder than finding Bertie.

He passed three skinny dogs snuffling through a garbage can that was lying on its side. They eyed Oliver with suspicion. But Oliver scampered past, his nose in the air. They had nothing to fear from him. He was not so hungry that he would eat trash. He had more pride than that. But he drank from puddles along the way because Bertie always let him.

Late in the day, when his feet were sore and his stomach aching, Oliver came upon Bertie's trail at last. It was just a hint of a smell at first, but as he ran, it grew stronger.

Baking bread! He pictured Bertie with flour up to her elbows. He felt the touch of her floury hand.

Scampering down a narrow street where the smell was strongest, he came to a shop where fat loaves of bread lay piled in a window. Oliver stuck his nose inside the door. He barked once, sharply, his signal for Bertie to come.

"Hey, pal." The human who was not Bertie knelt and patted Oliver's head. "You look like you've lost your best friend."

Oliver felt like weeping, but dogs seldom cry in the presence of strangers. Then he had his first really sad thought.

What if he never found Bertie? What then?

A Dress as Blue as the Sky

Maggie had thought she'd finished her dusting hours before, but here she was under Madame's bed, dusting again. Pushing up a corner of the satin bedskirt, she peered out. To her great surprise, what did she see but two skinny ankles. The ankles were connected to a pair of bare feet with crooked toes and long yellow toenails.

Madame shrieked as Maggie slithered out from under the bed. Madame's scrawny arms went up over her head. "Get out! Get out of here!" She grabbed a pillow and began pummeling Maggie's head as she raced for the door. "Out! Get out!" she shrieked.

Maggie raced along the corridor, down the stairs, and into the serving hall before stopping to catch a breath. She had seen Madame in her underclothes! With bare feet and bare arms! Maggie had never before seen Madame in anything but full dress. The wonder of it!

Madame's underskirts were made of something shiny and soft looking. Maggie thought it must be silk. How many silkworms, she wondered, did it take to make one underskirt? How many to make a whole dress? How did you get the silk from silkworms anyway? Could worms be milked like cows?

"You are not ready!" cried Hannah. Lifting the skirts of her best gray dress, she swiftly crossed the stone floor. On her head was the little white maid's cap Maggie hated because it looked just like a muffin. "Quickly, now! The musicians have taken their place. The duchess will be here any minute."

She pushed Maggie in the direction of the maids' quarters. "And remember, girl, not a word. Keep your eyes straight ahead and your tongue in your mouth."

Maggie went to the closet where the good dresses hung, washed and ironed and gray as the dust clinging to her hair. She wished just once in her life for a dress that was not brown or gray. A blue dress, the color of the sky on a summer's afternoon.

She washed her face and combed her unruly hair. She put on her gray dress and tied on a clean white apron. Last, without looking into the glass, she plunked the muffin cap onto her curly brown hair.

She raced downstairs and into the grand salon. As the musicians played a merry tune, she took her place next to Hannah in the long line of maids standing with hands clasped.

Not one said a word, not one sniffed or sneezed or breathed. Tall windows looked on with glazed indifference, and the drapery sulked. They had seen it all and cared for none of it.

At last, there came the sound of carriage wheels and a driver's "Ho, now!"

A horse snorted. A man spoke in a low tone, a woman answered. Madame said, "Your Highness," her voice an octave higher than usual. The duchess was coming!

Maggie could not contain her excitement, or her curiosity. She sneaked a peek down the line.

Madame led the way into the room. She was dressed in green, her hair piled up like a raisin bun. She held her chin high, and Maggie could see that it wobbled the tiniest bit. For all her riches, Madame Dinglebush was as nervous as a house maid.

There came another delicious rustle of skirts, and

in stepped the Duchess of Landsaway. Maggie remembered to avert her eyes, but not before she had seen three amazing things.

First, the duchess was very old and very short, not much taller than a child of ten-going-on-eleven.

The second most amazing thing was the color of her dress. It was as blue as a summer sky.

Maggie longed to look again, but she could hear Madame coming, chattering like a magpie. She was leading the duchess and her entourage past the maids and straight toward Maggie.

Maggie held her breath and bit her tongue to keep it still.

Madame passed, the skirt of her green dress rustling grandly. And there, before Maggie's wide eyes, was the duchess and the third most amazing thing: she had the sweetest, saddest face. It was as if something terrible had once happened that she could never forget.

Could terrible things happen to rich people? Could rich people feel sad, just the way poor people did? Did they cry, just as poor people sometimes cried? How she longed to ask the duchess.

Then the duchess did the most extraordinary thing: she turned her head and smiled straight at Maggie.

"Oh, Duchess!" said Maggie, unable to stop herself. "You have the most beautiful dress!"

Madame whipped around so fast that her ruffles nearly tripped her. "Who said that?"

Maggie's face turned bright red.

Madame's lips trembled, her eyes blazed with angry fire.

"I told you! What did I tell you? Now you've done it!"

In the kitchen, Hannah bustled from plate to plate, wiping away a drip of gravy, adding a sprig of parsley. "You just watch that door. Madame will be coming through it with a switch any minute!"

But it was not until the duchess and her party had left for the evening that Madame finally appeared.

She did not look angry. She smiled at Maggie, but the smile was laced with vinegar.

"The help find me—what shall I say?—unkind at times, I'm afraid," said Madame. "But I am not an uncharitable woman. I took you in, little snippet, when others might have sent you to an orphanage. Do you know what life is like there?"

Maggie slowly shook her head.

Madame's black eyes snapped and sparked. "No, of course you don't. I took you in. Fed you, clothed you, gave you a bed to sleep in. And how have you repaid me for my kindness? With insolence! With disobedience! Well, I will not have it."

"I am sorry, Madame," said Maggie, whose tongue felt as heavy as meat pudding. "I will never speak again, I promise."

"No," said Madame, coldly, "I do not believe you will. Not under this roof."

Turning to Hannah, she said, "I wish never to lay eyes on this girl again. I trust you know what that means."

Hannah wrung her hands together. "Madame, I . . . Madame, please. She has no one—"

"Nor do you, as I remember." Madame pushed a long, skinny finger into Hannah's chest. "Shall you leave together?"

Hannah's eyes widened in fear. "Oh, no, ma'am. Please, ma'am!"

"Then do as I say." With a final swirl of her taffeta skirts, Madame departed the kitchen.

A Shadow on the Snow

As darkness settled over the city, snow began to fall. Oliver lifted his nose and caught some snowflakes on his tongue, then more. It had been a long day of searching, and he was thirsty.

He had found nothing. Not Bertie, not food, nothing. Maybe he was not part bloodhound after all. Maybe he was mostly spaniel or—he shuddered—*poodle*.

He put his nose to the street for one last try, but the snow was beginning to pile there. This was truly a cold trail.

It was time to find shelter. In the morning, after a good night's sleep, he would start again.

Shivering in his thin coat, Oliver padded through the snow. Yellow light from windows high above poured out onto the snow, but he was just a small, dark shadow that no one saw.

A fancy carriage passed, drawn by four black horses. The horses snuffed and snorted and blew white clouds into the air. The bells on their harnesses jingled like Christmas. In the carriage sat an old woman so small she could barely look out into the street. On her head was a blue hat the color of a summer sky. When she saw Oliver, she smiled and waved a tiny hand.

It was not Bertie, but Oliver wagged his tail just the same. And, for a little while, he felt warm inside.

He tried not to think about his rug. As far back as he could remember, when evening came, Bertie would sit by the hearth while the fire blazed and Oliver snoozed on his rug. He had thought warmth would always be his. He had taken it for granted. He had taken everything for granted: his rug, his bowl filled with food, his baths, the soft hand that rested lightly on his head.

Bertie had told him how special he was. Did he not deserve special things? Did he not, at least, deserve to be warm?

So deep in memory was Oliver that the figure on one knee before him made him leap away.

"Hey, old chum," said the man who had eyes like Gerd, but who wasn't Gerd. He reached out and Oliver sniffed his fingers, which had traces of meat juice on them. Then he could not help himself. He licked the stranger's hand.

"Where's home, fella? Your folks must be looking for you. Get along home now, before the weather turns nasty." The stranger stood, walked to the curb, stepped up into an automobile, and, in a cloud of smoke, disappeared.

Oliver looked up into the night sky as flakes of snow swirled around him. The stranger was right about one thing: the storm was getting worse. But he was wrong about the other thing. No one was looking for Oliver, no one at all.

Just a Pile of Rags

Maggie stood on the stone stoop of Madame's fine house and looked out into the snow. The whole world was beautiful, so clean and white that she forgot for just one moment to be afraid.

Madame's door was shut and locked behind her. She had heard the bolt go through, a scary sound when you are on the other side of it. Hannah had locked the door. But Madame had ordered it. What else could Hannah do?

Did Madame see the small bundle Hannah had quickly pushed into Maggie's hands along with her coat and scarf? Maggie did not think so. No food left Madame's house without her orders.

Maggie did not like orders. She did not like orders, and she asked too many questions. It was her own fault that she was standing on a cold stoop in her threadbare coat on a winter's night. She was ten years old, and she ought to have known better. Now she would have to make her own way in the world. She did not know how a ten-year-old girl went about doing that, but she was determined to find out.

She would have to find employment, that was certain. It should not take long. After all, she could dust and polish as well as any housekeeper twice her age. She made the neatest bed without a bit of help.

Other things she did less well. But that was only because she could not keep her mind on them. Who wanted to shovel ashes from the hearth when the sun was shining, or when a kitten needed to be held and stroked under the chin?

Maggie gazed wide-eyed at the grand houses as she passed them, each more elegant than the one before. As the cold crept through the thin scarf tied under her chin, she turned up the walkway of the next-to-last house on the block. Its door was so tall that Maggie nearly toppled over backward trying to see where it ended.

In the middle of the door, higher than she could reach, was a polished brass knocker in the shape of a lion's head. With stiff fingers curled into a fist, Maggie knocked at the door.

And knocked.

And knocked.

No one answered.

At the last house, a short, fat butler appeared at once. "Yeeees?" he said, and Maggie was heartened by the twinkle in his eye.

But when she asked for work, he said there was none. She should take herself home at once, he said. A storm was coming. A person her size could be covered in snow in a matter of hours and disappear altogether.

"Altogether!" he said, his eyes wide, as if he could see her disappearing already.

Maggie hurried across the street and up a long drive to a house all covered in ivy, but there, too, no one was needed. She began to feel afraid.

Where would she sleep if she had no work? Where would she find food? Hugging her warmth in, she hurried up the street.

A brown dog with hair like a scrub brush came loping up behind her. Maggie nearly leapt out of her skin, but the dog went on its way, making a wet, clean line through the snow with its nose.

Fine homes gave way to small houses, and then ramshackle houses, and Maggie walked on.

Night was beginning to fall. A lamplighter reached up with his long stick to light the streetlamps. The pools of light that lay on the snow all down the street seemed to be leading her somewhere.

Shivering, Maggie stopped at the door of a bar and grill. The door opened, and out came noise along with two men. They were laughing heartily and patting their large stomachs. Before the door could close behind them, Maggie dashed in.

The place was filled with people. Smoke hung in a cloud. A man was beating notes out of a piano. A lady with a big red hat was singing at the top of her lungs. A serving girl, holding a tray full of foaming glasses high above her head, went through the crowd.

The big, smoke-filled room was warm, that was the best thing. Maggie found a corner to sit in and opened the sack Hannah had given her.

Inside was a piece of bread spread with a thin layer of goose fat. Taking the stingiest nibble to make the bread last, Maggie felt her first stab of homesickness. She had always considered Hannah family, her only bit of family in the world.

What did one do without family?

But what was this beneath the bread? A bit of gold? A coin? No. A heart. A tiny golden heart on a chain, a locket that opened to reveal a picture of a dark-haired lady.

Maggie almost dropped it. The locket did not belong to her. What was it doing in her sack? Hannah wouldn't have put it there. Hannah owned nothing this fine. As she often said, she was "as poor as a church mouse."

Had the locket slipped from Madame's dresser and somehow fallen into the little sack? It did not seem possible, but neither did the fact that Maggie had it in her hand. She glanced quickly around the room to see if anyone was watching. She could be arrested for stealing something as fine as this locket. She dropped it into her sack and felt within her the anxious beating of her heart.

But she couldn't stop thinking about it. Maybe Hannah meant her to have the golden locket. Maybe Hannah had stolen it from Madame! Would she have done that? Maggie didn't think so. Hannah was terrified of Madame, as was everyone else in the house.

So maybe the locket did not belong to Madame, but to someone else. But whom? The dark-haired lady?

Maggie's nimble mind hatched another thought: Hannah was saying with this locket something she could not tell Maggie while Madame watched. "Sell this!" she might have said. Or something else. But what?

Besides Madame, only Hannah remembered the day that Maggie was taken in. "Poor, unfortunate thing" was all she'd say whenever Maggie asked about her beginnings. Maggie had thought Hannah meant that the poor, unfortunate thing was herself, but what if it was someone else?

The dark-haired lady.

Maggie reached into the sack, took out the locket, and opened it once again.

Could it be? Could the lady in the locket be— Maggie almost couldn't ask it—her own mother?

But how could this beautiful lady be Maggie's mother? As Hannah reminded her often enough, Maggie was nothing more than a pudding-faced imp. God gave her brains, but not much else.

With her fingers curled tightly around the locket and her mind buzzing with unanswerable questions, Maggie curled into a corner of a warm booth. Maybe her dreams would deliver the answer she so desperately hoped for.

Clang! Clang!

"Last call!" yelled a fat man in a white shirt standing behind the bar. People began to leave, calling good night to friends. Head down, eyes closed, Maggie tried to make herself invisible.

"What's this? A pile of rags, is it?"

Maggie felt herself being lifted by the back of her coat. Then she was staring straight into the round red face of the man in the white shirt.

"Not rags, no, sir," said Maggie.

"And where is your family, child? Did they go and leave you behind?"

"No, sir. I've got no family. Well, there's Hannah, but Madame's door is locked and—"

"And you've got no place to go." The red-faced man set Maggie on the floor and shook his head. He sighed through his nose. "Well, I can't very well throw you out into the cold," he said. "You wouldn't survive the night, the bit of a thing that you are. Come on, then." He turned his back to Maggie and bent over so that she could climb on. "The missus will be waiting up."

Maggie laid her head against the man's warm back and barely felt the snow gathering on her neck as they crossed the street.

"Oh, Walter, not another one!"

The man let Maggie slide from his back. The missus looked her over like a dog sniffing.

"For the one night, my darling, that's all," said Walter.

"It had better be," said his wife. "We have nothing more to share. This child will steal the food from the mouths of your own children."

"But I wouldn't!" cried Maggie, horrified. "I would never!"

"For the one night," Walter repeated, looking down at Maggie's little face with sorrow drawn on his own. "For the one night, that's all. I promise."

A Bone of One's Own

In his cave of snow-covered bushes, Oliver awoke, frozen from nose to tail. Had he turned overnight into one of Gerd's ice blocks? If he waited, would Gerd come and snatch him up? Would he be delivered to Bertie's so he could thaw out by Bertie's fireplace, sleeping warmly at Bertie's slippered feet?

But Oliver knew, even in his half-awake frozen state, that there was something a bit off in his thinking. A dog could not be turned into a block of ice, no matter how cold he felt. And Bertie was not sitting by her fireplace waiting for him to come home.

Sometime during the night, Oliver had dreamed about a bird. It was a strange dream for a dog to have, especially for a dog who would rather eat a bird than dream of one. The bird was huge and white, the color of newly fallen snow, and as it hopped along, it waved a wing for Oliver to follow. Oliver followed, first walking, then loping, then racing as the bird ran faster and faster.

"Wait!" the dreaming Oliver cried, he didn't know why. What did he want with a silly old bird anyway? Faster and faster Oliver ran until the bird, without seeming to try, lifted its giant wings and took to the air.

It was Bertie! The giant white bird was his Bertie!

"Come back! Come back!" he cried, but Bertie kept flying up and up until at last she disappeared into the white sky.

He thought about his dream now. He did not know the meaning of it, only that he must keep looking for his best-in-all-the-world friend.

Groaning like an old dog, which he was not, he got slowly to his feet and gave himself an all-over shake. A good shake always made things better. Made his blood wake up, for one thing. For another, a good shake always set you up to do whatever you had in mind to do. It said, "Go to it, boy."

Why humans hadn't figured that out was a mystery to him.

But he was still hungry, dizzy hungry, and the air had no food smells in it, no trail to follow. He put his nose to the ground and at once sneezed out snow.

Eat first, search later. Bertie would understand. She would have to wait just a little longer.

The city had begun to awaken from its cold sleep. Windows opened, water splashed onto the street and into the gutter. One human called a greeting to another. An arm reached out to pull from a clothesline a pair of frozen long johns. A child began to howl. Wagon wheels creaked, and a horse nickered.

Gerd's wagon? Oliver's ears lifted, and a little cry escaped his throat. He ran to sniff the wagon. It was not Gerd's. This wagon was piled high with rags that smelled of many lives and the many things that had happened in those lives.

To a dog of Oliver's sensitivities, the odor was foul, and he turned his nose away.

"Hey, doggie!"

A young boy fat in his winter clothes threw a red ball at Oliver. The ball bounced once and rolled down the street.

"Get it, doggie!" yelled the boy, pointing.

But Oliver ran on, stopping only to sniff the ball as he went.

He ran more quickly now, more desperately, as the ache in his empty belly began talking to him: *Feed me! Get to it, boy!*

Back he went, into the square where the stalls were filling with every imaginable thing—pastries and breads, fruits and vegetables, trussed chickens being pushed onto sticks and set over flames.

Oliver knew better than to try that stall again.

He wound his way through the people crowding into the square and moving slowly from one stall to the next. They poked at the food, sometimes staying to buy.

A man with huge red hands, wearing a white apron streaked with blood, passed Oliver with great long strides. He was chewing on a meaty bone, grease dripping from his chin and down his neck.

Oliver walked in the man's wide shadow. He was trying to feed his stomach with the rich smell of that meat when, to his astonishment, the bone landed at his feet.

Oliver snatched it up and ran, ready to guard his prize to the death.

Food! His own bone!

He loped along until he came to the wide-open

water where the fishing boats were docked and great steamships bellowed. He took his precious bone to the place where an immense bridge touched the shore and happily, gratefully, began to chew.

Life got no better than this.

Well, it did. But that would mean that he had found Bertie, which he surely would before this day was done.

If Only

As she did every morning, Maggie pinched herself awake. It was still dark, so dark she did not
at first remember where she was or how she'd come
to be there. She had thought that she lay in her bed
at Madame's house and that the breathing, the little
snuffles and snorts in the room, came from her fel-
low maids.

Which was of course the reason for the pinch. She
could not get herself up otherwise. Instead, she
would lie abed and listen to the *hoo-hoo*ing of her
owl. She would daydream of her someday life, a life
not of luxury but of certain simple pleasures,

comfortable ladylike shoes, a hair ribbon or two, a best friend, time to herself.

Perhaps even a book.

Yes. How wondrous it would be to own a book. Hannah, who had gone to school as a child, taught Maggie to read, but their only book was the Holy Bible. Maggie thought she might like a book about animals—animals and birds.

But this was not a time for daydreaming about books, or anything else.

Quietly she rose from her pallet, folded the blanket, and, as the sun sent in its first rays, got into her clothes.

The door creaked as she opened it. Maggie froze, but no one stirred. Casting a backward glance at the five small sleeping figures, Maggie, step by careful step, made her way down the worn wooden stairs. No stealer of food from other children's mouths was she. She would starve first.

Reaching into her little pouch, she took a nibble of her bread. Then, because she could not help herself, another.

Strange how the more she ate, the hungrier she became. Why was that? Was it true for everyone, or just herself? And was it true at all, or just a figment of what Hannah called her "overblown imagination"?

But this was not a time for aimless wondering, either. Sadly, it never was. Gazing for a moment at her precious locket, Maggie put her crust of bread inside her pouch.

If only she could stay and thank Walter. He had saved her life. What had she to give him in return but her words? Nothing. Yet if she stayed until he awoke, what trouble she would make for him. He would insist that she eat a bite of breakfast, and she could not. She would not.

She may be no more than a pudding-faced imp, but she had never been a thief, and she would not be one this day.

As the sun lit up an amber-colored square of glass in Walter's kitchen window, Maggie slipped out the door and into the frosty morning. A snowflake, then another, floated lazily to the earth.

And there went that same brown dog, or what appeared to be the same dog as yesterday, scooting along with its nose to the ground. What a strange creature, searching for food along an icy sidewalk.

What kind of dog was he anyway? Where did he live? What was his name?

Taking care not to slip, Maggie began to follow the dog. Some dogs were smarter than people. Perhaps he knew something she did not.

Tucking her hands into her armpits, she ducked her head and hurried along. If only she had mittens.

Another good pinch was due. Once the "if onlies" began, there would be no end to them. If only she had a family, if only she were bigger or stronger or older or prettier or smarter.

See? And that was just the beginning.

Better to count the blessings that she did have, which was easier in its way. The list was short, shorter now that she no longer had Hannah or a bed or meals or a position with Madame Dinglebush. There was her coat, her woolen socks (which could be counted as two blessings), her boots (also two) with good soles, one well-made gray dress, her necessaries, the mysterious locket, and a crust of bread smeared with goose fat.

Nine blessings. Nearly two hands' worth.

The dog had found its way to an open marketplace. Men with broad, flat shovels were clearing last night's snow. Stalls were being hung with banners and signs, and set with food and wares.

Perhaps she could be an apple seller. How hard could that be?

Just ahead she saw the brown dog pounce upon a bone dropped by a butcher and take off like he had stolen it.

Maggie wandered over to the apple stall. How brilliantly red the apples looked in the drabness of a winter's morning.

"Fancy an apple, do ye, lass?" said the tall, thin man with snaggleteeth and bright green eyes.

"I do, yes. But I have no money. Do you have some work for me? I can peel apples as fast as—as a dog takes off with a bone."

"Can ye, now? Well, that would be no good to me, little one. We make no pies here. You might try that woman over there." He pointed to a stall draped in red and white.

Maggie took a last lingering glance at the apples. "Thank you, sir," she said, and crossed the square. The sky was white and the air was still, but the snow had stopped.

The woman at the red-and-white stall had a smushed-up face and narrow eyes. Seeing Maggie coming, she turned away.

Maggie spoke to the woman's back, telling the woman all the things she had learned to do at Hannah's elbow, not the least of which was rolling a perfect piecrust.

"Get on with you, now," the woman said over her shoulder. "I've got no work for you."

She tried another stall and another, getting

nothing for her efforts until the very last one. There she was given some bits of biscuit but, alas, no work.

"Take yourself over to the shirtwaist factory, corner of Fortune and Down," said the baker. "They'll give you work."

"Thank you, sir," said Maggie.

Work! She was in luck. The factory would give her work, he said. Not even a perhaps. He seemed to know. Thanking Hannah belatedly for her sewing lessons, Maggie left the marketplace and headed in the direction the baker pointed.

Not one day out of her position at Madame's and she had found work.

Well, almost. She hurried on, confidence like buttered toast with jam sitting inside her.

But where was Fortune Street? Down Street? She looked for a friendly face, then an almost-friendly face, then settled for a sleepy-looking face inside a checkered kerchief. "Please, ma'am, could you tell me how to find the shirtwaist factory on the corner of Fortune and Down?"

The sleepy face awoke. Its eyes widened. "What do you want with the factory?" the woman said.

"Work," said Maggie, simply.

"Not there," said the woman. "You don't want to work there."

"I don't?"

"Not if you value your health," said the woman.

Maggie valued her health, all right. As much as any child can, which is not to think about something so easily come by. "Please, ma'am. If you can tell me."

The woman sighed and shook her head. "Two blocks left, three blocks right, and you shall find it," she said. "God help you."

Speak

The building on Fortune and Down was ever so tall. Maggie looked up and up, and there at last was the top of it pushing smugly into the white sky. Maggie found her way to the door, brass hinges and dark wood, four times her height. She pulled at the door with all of her strength, but to no avail.

Was there no one working here after all?

Just then a panel truck painted with the words CRAWFORD AND SONS, PURVEYORS OF FINE CLOTHING rounded the corner and came to a stop at a door in the side of the building.

Maggie dashed down Fortune Street, up the steps, and through the open door.

The room she entered was dimly lit. In long rows sat women of every size and age bent over their sewing or pushing fabric through clacking machines. Faint light from dust-coated windows fell softly on their heads.

Beside each woman, clothing cut but unsewn waited in tall stacks. No one looked up.

"Excuse me," said Maggie. She cleared her throat and said louder, "Excuse me."

"Hold your water," said a voice from the back of the room. "I'll get to you in a bit."

Maggie watched a woman big with child using her belly to sew upon. The woman looked weary, though it was still morning.

Then Maggie's eyes lit upon a boy that she had at first taken for a short, thin woman. In all of her life, she had never seen a boy sew. How strange. Where had he learned? Were his hands as capable as any girl's? What was he doing here? How old was he?

But stranger than a sewing boy was the fact that no one spoke. Except for the occasional "pass me this" or "gimme that," the place was bereft of human speech; except for the occasional sigh, quite empty of human emotion.

Well, work was nothing to laugh about. Maggie didn't expect humor, but even the maids jollied about when Madame was out of hearing. They told each other stories, true ones and not-so-true ones, sometimes wicked ones. They kept each other entertained while they worked.

As far as Maggie could tell, there would be no stories in this place. Difficult as it would surely be, Maggie would be forced into silence.

If she'd learned anything from her last day with Madame, it was to hold her tongue.

A man wearing a cobbler's apron came clunking toward her, leaning on a cane. Maggie found herself staring at a shoe tied onto a block of wood.

Looking up from the shoe, she found two impatient, dark eyes waiting. "Well, what's it to be, girl? A handout or honest work?"

"Honest work, sir!" said Maggie at once.

The man picked at his teeth with a little stick. "How old are you? And don't lie to me. It makes no difference."

"Ten, sir. Eleven on my next birthday."

"You don't say."

"I do, sir."

"I've got work for you," he said. "I've got work for anybody who wants honest work. Six-day workweek, off on the Sabbath." He pointed at her nose. "Providing you work until the last bell and ask no questions."

"No, sir. I mean, yes, sir."

"And when the authorities come, you and the boy there"—he pointed at the sewing boy, who glanced up and went back to his work—"quick, jump into that bin." His finger went to a box filled with scraps of cloth. "There's a law about hiring brats like you, and I don't want no trouble."

"No, sir," said Maggie. "I mean, yes, sir. I'll jump straight into that bin."

"No food on premises. No chatter. Fifteen minutes for the midday break. One minute past, and you'll be fined."

"Yes, sir," said Maggie. "I mean, no, sir. I won't be late."

"See that you are not," he said. "Name's Speak, Nicholas Speak. That's 'Mr. Speak, sir' to you."

Maggie held out her hand. "My name is Maggie Street," she said. "I shall be happy to work for you, Mr. Speak. Sir."

Speak grabbed her hand quite roughly and pulled her along behind him. "We'll see what you're worth, girl." He led her to a table piled high with shirtsleeves waving for help. Or so it appeared.

Maggie had a million questions for Mr. Speak. Where was the washroom? for one. What would she be paid for her work? "Mr. Speak? Sir?"

"No chatter," he said. "Apply yourself. I will be checking your work."

From his apron pocket he took a spool of white thread and a needle. "After this, you provide your own," he said.

"Yes, sir," said Maggie.

Where did one purchase thread and a needle? She didn't dare ask.

She had been given a table in the dimmest part of the room and a stool that had once been a chair.

Such a sinking feeling in the pit of her stomach.

Why was that? She had found employment, and in less than one day.

Well, she was hungry, that's all. It would pass.

She slipped her hand into the sack where the locket was, and for a little while felt filled to the brim with something more precious than food.

Mercy

With his paws wrapped around his precious bone, Oliver gnawed and gnawed until no evidence existed that meat had ever been upon it. Then he dug the bone a nice deep hole and buried it.

Coming out from beneath the bridge, he began wandering along the wet, pebbled shore, stopping to sniff an oyster shell, fish bits, an orange rind, then a place where another dog had been. He looked out across the water that seemed to have no end.

For some reason that he did not know, the water buoyed his spirits.

And then he did know.

One day when Oliver was still a pup, Bertie had come home with this same water smell clinging to her skirt. Her cheeks were pink and her eyes filled with something that Oliver had seen only in the eyes of children.

Excitement, he guessed it was. Pleasure.

She had taken from her pocket a photograph of a man standing on the deck of a boat—a stiff-looking man, Oliver thought, but Bertie seemed to like him all the same. She gazed at the photograph for a long while before placing it along with a flower between the pages of her black book.

Oliver's memory had given him a clue. Bertie was here, here with the stiff-looking man among these boats. Oliver had only to find either one of them and his search would be over. Bertie would throw her arms around his middle, and Oliver would be so happy that he would beat her unmercifully with his tail.

Well, he wasn't at all happy that she had left without telling him where she was going or when she would be back. But he would forgive her, and life would go on the way it was. The way it always had been and was supposed to be.

Was that too much to expect?

Once, Bertie had offered Oliver a bite of her fish from her plate. Perch, she called it. Oliver had sniffed at the perch, and because he did not know then, as often we do not, that food might not always appear so magically, he turned it away.

Now, famished, smelling that same strange smell, his mouth began to water.

All along the dock, fishermen were readying their boats, pulling down nets and floats, washing their decks so that fishy-smelling water spilled out onto the shore.

Impatient, Oliver ran up the gangplank of the first boat he came to. From below came the sounds of human activity, but the deck for the time being was his. He searched it thoroughly, bloodhoundingly. Not a bite of perch was to be found, much less a trace of Bertie.

Oliver's nose had done its job, but his ears had let him down, for suddenly right above him stood a giant of a man, his fists on the waist of his rubber trousers.

"What have we here?" said the man in a booming voice.

Just as Oliver was about to bolt, the big man dropped to one knee beside him and grabbed the scruff of his neck.

The man had trustworthy eyes. "Lost are ya, fella?" he said. "Where's your master?"

He began scratching Oliver behind the ears. Oliver swooned. "I've got nothing for ya, boy. But stick around awhile, and we'll see what we can fetch from the sea. How's that?"

Out of all those strange words, Oliver picked the one he knew: *fetch*. Fetch was a game he'd played with Bertie's grandson. So when the big man pulled in the ropes and went up into a little house above the deck, Oliver stuck around.

Only when the deck rumbled under his feet and the water began to churn did Oliver have second thoughts. But by then, it was too late. Sliding and scrambling from one side of the deck to the other, Oliver was going out to sea.

Miss Fancy Coat

By the time the midday bell rang, Maggie's eyes were tired. She had been staring for hours at her needle in the near dark. Three times she had poked that needle toward her finger, pulling back in the nick of time.

If she'd bloodied a cuff or a sleeve, what then?

No job, that's what.

All around her, women were rising from their chairs, stretching their backs against their hands, yawning, groaning, moving like cattle toward a door in the back of the room.

And now they were talking, all of them, all at once.

"Hazel! Yoo-hoo!" called one. "Save me a place next to you. Have I got a story!"

"My fool of a son," said another. "You won't believe what he's up to!"

An elderly lady, bent nearly in half, stopped at Maggie's table. "Come along now, child," she said. "You have only a quarter hour. You don't want to waste it."

Maggie jumped up and followed, last in line.

The room used for work breaks was small and airless. The women crowded in, taking food out of sacks for their midday meal.

Maggie climbed into a small space between the old woman and a younger woman with flaming red hair. Across the table sat the sewing boy. His hair was the color of hay and stuck out all over his head. Chewing on an apple, he stared at Maggie with hard eyes.

"Where d'you come from?" he said. "You with your fancy coat."

Maggie looked down at her coat as if seeing it for the first time. Fancy? The gray coat with its big black buttons had once belonged to Madame's granddaughter. Maggie appreciated the coat for its warmth, but she hadn't thought it fancy.

"Leave the child be, Danny," said the red-haired woman beside her. "She's not been here one day and you with your nasty mouth!"

"Huh!" said the boy called Danny, wiping a sleeve across his apple-wet mouth. "Just 'cause you're my big sis, don't think you can—"

"Shut it," said his sister. "The less we hear from you, the better."

The chatter, which had stilled, started up again. Maggie slipped her hand into her little pouch and drew out her crust of bread.

The red-haired girl looked down, her eyebrows raised. "That's all you've got?"

Maggie nodded.

"Here, then," said the girl. "I don't care much for apples."

The apple was not one of those she had seen in the market. This one was green with mushy brown spots, but for Maggie it was a true gift. Gifts came seldom in her life.

"Oh! Thank you!" she said.

The red-haired woman shrugged. "Ain't nothin'," she said. "We help each other out when we can. Don't we, girls?"

A half dozen women around the table nodded or said "we do" or "when we can."

A shy smile tugged at the corners of Maggie's mouth. The room filled with bodies was stifling, but now the warmth was welcome. She was beginning to think the factory might not be such a bad place when the bell clanged and the women got up from the table.

"Back to work. No dawdling," ordered Nicholas Speak, appearing out of nowhere.

Maggie was last in line, except for one person: Danny the sewing boy. Skimming past her into the big room, he whispered, "Stick with me, girl. These old biddies don't know nothin'." He stuck out his hand. "The name is Daniel Durch, and I ain't afraid of nothin' or nobody."

Maggie shook his hand. "Maggie Street," she said. But that's all she said, because she *was* afraid of some things and some people. Nicholas Speak, for one.

"I'll show ya the ropes," said Daniel Durch.

"What ropes?" said Maggie, looking around her.

"It's a sayin'," he said. "Don'tcha know nothin'?"

"I know about some things," said Maggie.

Daniel smirked. "Like what?"

"Owls," said Maggie, the first thought that came to her.

Daniel frowned. "Owls?"

"Yes," said Maggie with great conviction. "Owls."

A Fine and Delicate Clue

As the big fisherman flung his net out onto the water, Oliver fought to keep his footing on the deck. Then up from below came another man. This one was smaller but just as strong. Together the two pulled in a net filled with squirming silver fish and dumped it onto the deck.

Oliver danced around as the fish swam through his legs. Soon they were scooped up into tubs and Oliver was left to lick the wet and empty deck.

An argument sprang up between the men. Oliver did not know what it was about. He knew only by their eyes that it had something to do with him.

Then the big one took a fish from a tub and sliced it open with his knife. Out came the fish's bones all in a piece. "Here you go, boy," he said, and gave the fish meat to Oliver.

Oliver did not need to be asked twice. In three bites, he finished that fish, asked for another, and got another.

This was his lucky day. He was sure to find Bertie this day. When the men were busy again at their net, Oliver went quietly below. There he found a tidy little room with cabinets and two narrow beds.

And Bertie!

Well, not in the flesh, but something of Bertie was here, or had been. Oliver put all his attention into sniffing, first along the floor, then along the beds, the smell of Bertie growing stronger as he went.

Digging his snout into a place where bed met cabinet, he found the source of the smell—a lady's white handkerchief.

Oliver tugged it out. Dropping the handkerchief onto the bed, he sniffed it all over. Bertie, all right.

But how could that be? The delicate handkerchief, bordered with blue forget-me-nots, was not one of hers. Bertie's handkerchiefs were all perfectly plain. They were stacked neatly in her dresser drawer, crisp and ironed. Each morning Bertie would take one out and douse it with her special water.

That was it! Bertie's special water was on the blue and white handkerchief.

If only he had human speech and could ask the fishermen.

As the boat rocked and another load of fish hit the deck above, Oliver stretched out on the floor, laid his snout on his paws, and tried to think. But the motion of the boat was too much for his poor brain and, along with the rest of Oliver, it fell asleep.

He awoke to a scratching sound. Picking up Bertie's handkerchief that wasn't Bertie's, Oliver went to investigate. The boat was back at the dock and the men were scrubbing the deck.

The big one looked up from his scrubbing. "Whatcha got there?" Frowning, he took the handkerchief from Oliver. Waving it at the other fisherman, he laughed. "This yours, Toby?"

"Nah, not mine, Ace," said Toby, whose face had grown red.

"Some lady friend, then?" said Ace.

"Nah, nothing like that. I found it on the street. Thought I'd give it to my old lady, but I forgot."

All this time, Oliver, understanding not one word, kept asking with his eyes, with his little yips, "Where's Bertie? Where did you put Bertie?"

Ace tied the handkerchief around Oliver's neck. "There you go, boy," he said. "It's yours now."

Both fishermen laughed. But after a bit they were arguing again.

"You know how I feel about dogs," Toby said. "Dogs don't belong on boats."

Oliver's ears went up at the word *dog*.

"This one's no trouble," said Ace. "But he's got a home somewhere, no doubt. Somebody waiting for him." He gave Oliver a last scratch behind the ears. "Out you go, boy."

"But where's Bertie?" said Oliver with his eyes.

"Shoo!" said Toby, chasing Oliver down the gang-plank and onto the dock.

As the gangplank rose, the sorrow of not having found Bertie took a bite out of Oliver's heart. He had come so close! What now?

He loped off down the dock, the handkerchief that was not Bertie's but that smelled like Bertie waving from his neck.

Golden Light

When the last bell of the day rang out, Maggie nearly fell off her stool. It was seven o'clock. For the past hour she had fought sleep, but at last her eyelids had fluttered and closed.

Now they opened wide, and her heart gave a lurch. Had Mr. Speak seen her fall asleep? Would this be her first and last day in the factory?

Her back was aching, her neck stiff from bending over one cuff and then another and another after that, so many that she had lost count. The minute one pile of sleeves and cuffs was finished, another appeared.

It was shortly after the midday break that Mr. Speak had whipped away one of her finished cuffs and taken it to his station. As she waited for his return, Maggie's fingers had trembled. But he did not come back.

Had she done well, or well enough? If she had not, would she be paid for the work she had done?

All around her, workers were tidying their stations. Tomorrow was the Sabbath, and the factory would be closed. A feeling of freedom danced through the stuffy air. One woman was humming, another smiled to herself, thinking perhaps of the Sunday meal she would prepare for her family or of a friend she might meet for tea.

Maggie straightened her station and put on her coat.

"Take your needle and thread, child," said the bent lady, passing Maggie's station. "Or someone will snatch them from you."

Maggie did as she was told. Then she followed the bent lady and all the other ladies down the aisle that led to the back door.

"Where d'ya live?"

Startled, Maggie turned around, and there was Daniel Durch with his hands stuffed into his pockets. Perched on his haystack hair was a flat cap with a small brim. His eyes searched Maggie's like a crow looking for food.

"I live—" Maggie was about to say that she lived with Madame Dinglebush. That of course would have been a lie, but to say she lived nowhere at all? That was somehow worse.

"I live in the Heights," she said primly.

"And I live with President Roosevelt!" scoffed Daniel Durch. "I'll bet a week's pay you got nowhere to stay at all. Ain't that right?" His beady dark eyes bored into hers.

"I do!" said Maggie. "There's my dog. Right over there." She pointed across the street to where that same brown dog was pushing his nose along the walkway. A bit of cloth was tied around his neck.

Daniel stood with his hands on his hips. "If that's your dog, why ain't he coming to you?"

"He will, in his own good time," said Maggie.

"Come on now, Danny," said his sister. "You know how Father is if you don't come right home. You don't want another whipping, do you?"

Daniel jutted his chin at the dog that had turned the corner and was heading up Down Street. "If that's your dog, you better call him," he said.

"Lucky!" called Maggie, the first name that came to her. To her great surprise, the dog stopped and turned his head.

Maggie clapped her hands. "Come here, Lucky! Come on, boy!"

The dog, a quizzical look on his face, came loping toward Maggie.

"I don't like dogs," said Daniel. Stooping, he picked up a rock and, before Maggie could stop him, flung it at the brown dog.

"No!" cried Maggie as the dog turned and ran.

"Daniel! You heard me," said his sister. "Get on home now."

"Stupid boy," said Maggie, but only to herself.

Daniel and his sister went down Fortune Street, so Maggie went the other way. Wherever she stayed the night, it would be as far from Daniel Durch as she could make it.

Unbeknownst to Maggie, who had spent the day indoors, the weather had turned warm. Some of the snow had melted, dripping from rooftops, sliding down into gutters, and winding its way at last to the sea.

Maggie meandered along the wet walkway with her hands in her pockets. She followed the water, which seemed to know where it was going.

The night was starless, but windows in houses along her way provided light. The light called Maggie to come inside, to warm herself, but the people did not.

For a time, cold is endurable. Hunger is endurable. Exhaustion is endurable. But not all at once. Not when you are ten going on eleven. At ten going on eleven, a child is meant to be curled into a chair by the fire, reading her favorite book, stroking a sleeping kitten. Someone should be bringing her a cup of hot cocoa and patting her curls, telling her what a special little girl she is.

That is how life is meant to be, but not always what it is.

But always there is something good.

Maggie stopped before a church with a tall steeple and windows like kaleidoscopes. Just then, the door opened and out stepped a man dressed in black robes. Around his neck was a starched white collar.

Maggie had never been in a church. Madame Dinglebush had her own prayer room into which the help crowded each Sunday. While the other maids slept through interminable sermons, Maggie's mind spun with all the questions she was never given the chance to ask. *Where exactly is God? What does He look like? Is He only good to people who are always good?* And the most perplexing question of all: *What if He isn't a He?*

Et cetera.

The man in robes and collar looked into the night

sky, then down at Maggie, who was looking at him. "Come inside for prayers, child," he said, opening the door behind him.

Maggie scurried up the steps and followed the priest through the doors and a small foyer into the light of the church, which was as golden as her locket. As the priest made his way up the aisle, Maggie stopped and looked up, up into a ceiling where immense winged angels, pink and blue and gold, swam through her vision. Never in her life had she seen anything so beautiful. Never had she felt so small.

She made her way to the end of the last pew and, bowing her head, began to pray.

Somewhere in the middle of her prayer, Maggie fell asleep.

Which was perfectly all right with God.

For the Love of a Poodle

Oliver felt terrible, the way you do when you've done something especially stupid.

It had been foolish to come to just anybody's call, especially if the human didn't even know your name. But Oliver had seen the little girl with the round blue eyes before somewhere.

Was it down by the docks? In the marketplace? Yes, he had seen her when he got his bone. Just now, she had called "Lucky!" and he, for some reason, had run to her and nearly gotten a rock to the head for his trouble.

He was slipping, no doubt about it. Strangers were not to be trusted. He knew that.

Well, he was lonely. With Bertie by his side all those years, he'd not known the meaning of the dark, sad feeling that lived inside him now. It was worse than hunger, that feeling, and he was all too ready to be rid of it.

He must be more careful. The girl was safe, but the boy she was with was not. Best to stay clear of them both.

His bone was where he'd left it, buried deep in the damp earth beneath the bridge. Oliver dug it up, sniffing it thoroughly end to end. Only the memory of meat remained, but he chewed it anyway because his teeth really wanted to.

By the time he was finished, Bertie's handkerchief that was not Bertie's was covered with mud and slobber. Bertie would be horrified when she saw it.

Of course, after first hugging him, she would untie the handkerchief and wash it. But what would she think of Oliver? She had taught him to be neat and tidy, given him weekly baths using her own French milled soap. The least he could do was keep the handkerchief clean. One day it would take its place among the plain ones in Bertie's dresser drawer. But first he would need to wash it.

Coming out from beneath the bridge, he poked his way along the shore. The night was dark, the air cold, but not as cold as the water. Oliver stepped out into it and at once began to shiver.

To heck with the silly handkerchief.

But it wasn't just the handkerchief. It was Oliver himself. He needed a bath. The handkerchief with its flowery smell was all he had to keep the fishy odor of himself from creeping into his nose.

He took another step and the water came up to his chest.

Enough!

Oliver splashed out of the water and up onto the shore, where he shook and shook himself. And then there was nothing left but the good smell of dog. He loped off in the direction of the marketplace.

Stopping along the way to examine a very dead mouse, he did not at first notice the white poodle. Wearing a bright red collar and leash, she was standing quite elegantly at her mistress's side, pretending to ignore the scruffy mutt making his way toward her.

Oliver scampered right up to the poodle. Their noses met, and Oliver was a goner. As he made his way to her other end, the poodle's mistress pulled her away.

"Stop, Henrietta!" cried her mistress. "Stop this ridiculous behavior!"

Up the stone steps went the lady, pushing Oliver

away with her booted foot and pulling Henrietta behind.

The door opened, then slammed shut, and Oliver stood panting on the other side.

What was happening to him? Had he fallen for a poodle? A mere poodle?

How could that be? One minute he was sniffing a dead mouse, and the next he was in love. It didn't seem fair. He hadn't been given any time at all to think about it. *Bam*, just like that, his heart said, "*Go.*"

Oliver stared at the door. He waited. He whimpered. A dog barked (was it her?). Oliver's heart danced into his throat. He listened with all of his senses. Time passed in its maddening way, slowly, slowly. Oliver lay before the door, his snout on his crossed paws.

Henrietta had to come out sometime. No dog could hold its water forever. If the poodle wanted him as much as he wanted her, she would be begging to come out.

But did she want him? *That* was the question.

Up the stone steps came a man wearing a black top hat and overcoat.

"Scoot," he said, pushing Oliver aside with his shiny black shoe. "Off you go!"

Oliver's first nibble of dog love left his tongue, and the bitter bite of loneliness returned.

All in Black

"Sit up, child. The service is about to begin."

A big woman dressed all in black and smelling of mothballs was poking Maggie's shoulder.

Maggie sat up and blinked herself awake.

"Churches aren't for sleeping, child. You're meant to worship in here, not sleep. Why, it's like thumbing your nose at Jesus!" She quickly crossed herself.

Thumbing her nose at Jesus? How terrible. But Maggie had been so very tired. She was sure Jesus would understand.

But just in case, she would never sleep all night in a church again.

She sat forward, straining her neck to see.

The priest who had let her in was walking up the aisle again. This time he was swinging a golden lantern with smoke pouring out of it.

Up ahead was a beautiful stage, a table spread with a gold and white tablecloth, and burning candles everywhere. There was soft, soft music coming from an organ that a lady played with her hands and feet all at the same time.

There were rows and rows of pews, and all of them were full of women with scarves or shawls over their heads and men without their hats on. The man in front of Maggie had a perfectly round bald spot that stared back at her like a sightless eye.

Maggie counted the people in her pew. Five women and three men, plus one tiny little woman at the end.

Maggie craned her neck around the mothball woman and stared.

The tiny woman was all in black. Long black skirt and coat, black boots buttoned onto tiny feet that didn't come near to touching the floor. Over her silver hair was a black lace shawl.

Was it the duchess? It was!

But why was she all in black? Had someone died? Her husband, the duke? Poor duchess!

Other women, like the woman right beside Maggie, wore black scarves, too. They couldn't all be widows, could they? Dare she ask? Instead, for the second time in just as many days, Maggie held her tongue.

Not one person in the whole church was talking. She thought there must be a rule. A rule against staring, too, but she couldn't help herself. The duchess was so small and so perfect. Only her tiny wrinkled face showed that she was a real person and not the doll she appeared to be.

Hers was a sad face, a sweet, sad face.

The face turned. Maggie's heart jumped. She blinked. She swallowed hard, and she kept on staring. She could not turn away from those bright blue eyes.

Nor, it seemed, could the duchess. But at last she did, closing her eyes and bowing her head in prayer.

The priest spoke, and all the people answered, their heads bowed. The woman beside Maggie played with a string of glass beads. Maggie quickly bowed her head.

The service went on forever, people standing, then kneeling, then sitting again. A boy laid a gold-and-white shawl around the priest's shoulders. The priest bent his head and kissed his own thumbs. Beneath the stage, candles in little red glasses flickered.

Maggie kept sneaking peeks at the duchess, who

never stood or kneeled. She just kept sitting with her head bent.

Why was that? Was there some different rule for duchesses?

And then Maggie figured it out: the duchess was asleep! There she sat, nice as you please, with her tiny hands folded and her eyes shut.

Was that a drop of drool sliding down her chin? It was! And was she snoring? She was!

Maggie giggled. She quickly clamped a hand over her mouth, but not before the lady beside her turned and scowled.

The duchess went right on snoring.

The service ended with a crashing of notes from the organ. People stood; the duchess awoke with a little smile. She stood and took the arm of a tall young man standing beside her.

Maggie followed them outside. At the curb stood the duchess's carriage, with its four black horses blowing their white breath into the air. The duchess made her way toward it alongside the young man, who patted the hand that rested on his arm.

Was the young man her son? His eyes were brown. Could a blue-eyed person have a brown-eyed son? Of course! Maggie's mother, if indeed the lady in the locket was her mother, had brown eyes, and Maggie's were blue.

There was so much Maggie didn't know, so much she wanted to know. What had happened to her mother? Had she given Maggie away? Was she sad, and did she cry to see her baby go? Was Maggie stolen from her arms?

Was Maggie even Maggie? Or did her mother name her something else?

And what about a father? Had she ever had a father?

And why was Madame the one to take her in? Why not somebody sweet and nice, like the tiny duchess?

Maggie watched as the duchess was helped into her carriage. The young man climbed in and sat beside her. The door was closed, and with a jangle of reins and a jingle of bells, off went the duchess.

Sunday in the Park with Oliver

In a small park, Maggie found a nice little bench set by a pond. A pair of mallards sailed past, eyeing her without seeming to, the way birds do. Overhead a flight of pigeons went on to someplace terribly important.

Taking out her crust of bread, Maggie nibbled until just a bit of it was left. She put the bit into her sack where the locket gleamed and hid its secret.

On the far side of the pond, Oliver watched the ducks. How hard would it be, he wondered, to nab a duck? He had never tasted duck, but it couldn't be worse than what he'd found in garbage cans.

Yes, he'd stooped that low. What else could a starving dog do?

Catching a duck meant going into the water again, getting Bertie's handkerchief that wasn't Bertie's wet again, and this water looked none too clean. He sniffed it, took a little taste, and sneezed it right out.

The ducks crossed the pond as if they were floating, not paddling furiously as they certainly were. That big, mean dog was up to no good.

Oliver, his nose to the dead grass, made his way slowly around the pond. His stomach was grumbling loudly and, no matter what he promised, it wouldn't shut up.

And there was that girl. She was sitting on a bench swinging her legs. Beside her was a dirty little pouch. Was there food inside it? Was it worth the risk? Sniffing the air, Oliver edged closer.

"Hey, Lucky!" cried the girl. She threw out her arms just the way Bertie did, as if he'd been gone forever and she was really happy to see him.

Oliver stopped. Was it a trick? Where was the boy?

The girl leaned forward and held out her hand. "Come here, Lucky. Come here, boy. I won't hurt you."

Her voice had music in it. Oliver went a step

closer. There was food in her pouch, he could smell it.

"You're hungry aren't you, boy?"

Oliver took another step.

The girl reached into her pouch, looked at the bite of bread that came out of it, and offered it to Oliver.

Oliver ran up and snatched it. One mash of his teeth, and the bread was gone.

"I wish I had something more for you," the girl said, "but I really don't." She turned the pouch inside out so that he could see. Something tiny and golden, like a bit of light, fell onto the ground.

"Oh!" The girl dropped to her knees. She stuck her head under the bench.

Couldn't she see the golden thing was right there next to her foot? Oliver went over and nosed it.

"You found it! You lovely dog!" The girl picked up the golden thing. Then she opened it and showed Oliver what was inside. "It's my mother," she said. "I think." She put the golden thing back inside the empty pouch and put the pouch in her pocket.

She reached for Oliver, and Oliver backed away.

"It's all right, boy," she said. "I would never hurt you." Her eyes had such sweetness in them.

He took a step toward the girl, then another. One

more, and she was patting his head, smoothing her hand down his back. Oliver shivered with delight.

"What's that you've got?" she said.

Kneeling beside Oliver, Maggie examined the lady's handkerchief around his neck. It was crumpled and dirty. Still, Maggie could see by the handkerchief's tiny stitches, its delicate blue flowers, that it had once been fine.

Whose dog was this? His mistress, no doubt, the lady who had owned the handkerchief. But when Maggie stood up to leave, the dog stayed beside her, and when she walked along the narrow paths of the park, he followed.

She didn't mind. It was good to have company.

Hunger made her light-headed, and it wasn't long before Maggie was sitting again, this time on a flat rock, the dog stretched out beside her. The sun, breaking through the sky's gray clouds, warmed them both, and they fell softly into sleep.

Maggie, weak with hunger, dreamed about Hannah's bread pudding, sprinkled with cinnamon and bursting with raisins.

Oliver dreamed about a meaty bone dripping grease.

The sun, unable to help, hid its face behind the clouds.

Maggie shivered and slid down off her cold rock to snuggle beside Oliver, who thought, for just a whiff of a second, that Bertie had come home.

I'm Not Lucky

Oliver awoke first. The girl lay beside him. She was breathing. At least, he thought she was. He gave her face a nice wet lick to make sure.

Maggie sputtered awake. She sat up, wiping dog spit off her face with her sleeve. "Hi, Lucky," she said, and patted his nose. She stood and began to brush the leaves off her coat and socks. Oliver gave himself a nice all-over shake.

Church bells near and far began to toll the time. Maggie knew it was early Monday morning, but she counted anyway. One, two, three, four. . . . no one had told her when to come to work, wasn't that odd? Five, six, seven.

She hurried out of the park and headed toward Fortune and Down, the dog at her heels.

She was in luck. As she rounded the corner, the factory's door was pushed open and the women began filing in.

Oliver watched the girl go up the steps and into the big building.

At the door, she turned and waved. "Bye, Lucky," she said.

His name was Oliver. Why didn't she know that? Lucky wasn't such a bad name, but it wasn't *his* name. As grouchy as his poor stomach, Oliver loped off in search of something to eat. Anything, at this point, with feathers or fins or, better yet, bones.

Oliver could feel his energy fading, falling behind him like a shadow. Even Henrietta, with all her beauty, could not compete with the hollow feeling that had dug a place inside him and would not leave. He must find food, and soon.

He made his slow way down to the harbor, but all the fishing boats were gone. An old black dog with its ribs showing shuffled through fish bones and mussel shells littered along the shore. It was a sad sight, and Oliver turned away.

Under the bridge, he dug up his bone and gave it a lick, but it brought him no joy. He left the bone behind, unburied. Maybe the old black dog would find some comfort in it.

Oliver looked out over the water, which ended in a flat, straight line. A boat with some cloth that caught the wind made its way straight toward that line. Oliver watched until the boat was out of sight, somewhere on the other side. Could Bertie be there? In that world beyond the line? Was it a better world? If so, why hadn't she taken Oliver with her?

Why had she left him behind? Here was the terrible question that Oliver had kept hidden from himself, just as he'd once hidden his bone. Bertie loved him, he was certain of that. She had fed him from her hand, pampered and petted him, bathed and walked him, read him stories from her little black book.

He couldn't understand the stories, but never mind. She did all the things a human does for a child. He had been her child.

And still, she left him. Without so much as a final pat, a teary good-bye.

And that is when Oliver knew, deep in the place in which the truest things are known, that he would never see Bertie again. Bertie was no longer in this world. Where she had gone, he might never know, but Bertie was not coming back, and he was never going to find her.

Partners

By midday break, the ache in Maggie's back was almost worse than the one that gnawed at her empty stomach. While the others took their break, she sat at her table holding her locket, opening and closing her hand to look at it all over again, each time a surprise.

When the others returned, she slipped the locket into her pouch and got back to work.

At seven, when the final bell rang, she laid her head on her table and closed her eyes.

"No sleeping on the job, you!"

Maggie bolted upright, but it was only Daniel Durch playing a dumb joke.

"You got no place to go, do you?" he said, his arms crossed over his skinny chest.

"Go away," she said.

"Come along, Danny!" called his sister from the door.

"I know where you can get something to eat," he said.

"Danny, you heard me!"

"You'd better go," said Maggie.

"Don't mind her," he said, jerking his thumb toward the door. "She ain't even going home. She's going to a party."

His sister left, arm in arm with another of the sewing girls.

"Come on," said Daniel. He motioned with his head. "I'm not foolin'. I know where there's food and plenty of it."

Maggie got up and put on her coat.

Oliver, who had gone three empty times to Henrietta's, was waiting by the back door for the girl he'd met at the pond, but when he saw her come out with the rock-throwing boy, he bolted off down the street.

"There goes your dog," said Daniel. "Good thing. I'd have beaned him."

Maggie scowled. "You are not a nice person."

"But what's it matter? I know where supper is."

Maggie's mouth watered at the mere mention of food. "Where?"

"You have to work for it. It's not free."

"All right," she said. "I don't mind. But if we find Lucky, you are not to throw any rocks."

"Deal," said Daniel.

Maggie followed Daniel down winding, cobbled streets, dark except for a bright window now and again. Tall brick buildings were pushed up against the street, leaving only a narrow, dimly lit walkway. Maggie splashed into one of the many puddles along the curb and got her boots soaked. A man dressed in rags wandered past on bare feet, muttering to himself.

Daniel strode ahead as if nothing could scare him, but when he turned into an alley, Maggie hesitated.

"Come on!" called Daniel over his shoulder. "The food will be gone if we don't get there fast."

A skinny black dog with yellow eyes slunk past Maggie. Behind her a voice bellowed, "Out! I said. Get out!" A door slammed. A woman with wild hair scurried down the alley wrapped in a blanket.

Maggie ran ahead to catch up with Daniel.

"It's right down here," he said. "I'll do the talking if there's any to be done."

They came to the one door in the alley that was

brightly lit, the back door of a dinner house. Kitchen sounds mixed with talk, and laughter erupted with the light. Daniel ducked his head in and out of the doorway. "The coast is clear," he said. "See what's in there," he said, nodding his head toward a wooden bin. "I'll keep watch."

In where? Maggie's eyes widened. Could he mean the garbage?

"Hurry up!" he said. "What are you waiting for? You're not afraid to get your hands dirty, are you?"

Maggie's mouth opened, then it shut. Her stomach tried in vain to move her feet.

"Big baby!" said Daniel when it was clear that Maggie wasn't about to do what he wanted. "You watch the door. I'll do the dirty work. *This* time."

But Maggie could not keep watch. Her eyes were glued to Daniel with his hands down inside the garbage. She watched him toss out a bone to which a hunk of meat was attached. "That one's for me," he said. "I'll find you one."

Maggie wanted to stop him, but her stomach wouldn't let her. Her stomach had no morals at all. It wanted Maggie to run right over and grab some meat for herself, and when Daniel tossed out another bone, that is exactly what she did. Then the two ran off down the alley like hungry, happy dogs.

Well, one happy dog and one not so happy.

They came to a bridge, an arched span black against a starry night sky. When they'd gone halfway across, Daniel stopped. Leaning his elbows on the rail, he tore off a chunk of meat with his teeth and began to chew. "I like to watch the boats at night," he said. Only it came out "Ilimptptowacbosneye" because his mouth was full. "I'm going to stow away on one of them boats and go to Australia," he said.

Maggie stared at her bone. She thought about Lucky. She would save the bone for him. But first she had to eat some of the meat. She had to, or she would starve to death.

It was awful, the thought of starving to death. Worse than the thought of chewing meat that somebody else had chewed on first.

She took a little nibble, then a bite, her stomach urging her on. She stopped when she was not quite full.

"What're you doing with that?" said Daniel, as Maggie tucked the bone inside her pouch.

"Saving it for Lucky," she said.

"For the stupid dog?" he said. "Here, let me have that!" He grabbed the pouch from Maggie and turned it upside down. Out fell the bone along with

Maggie's locket. She dove for the locket, but Daniel came up with it first.

"Holy Mother!" he said, with a low whistle. "We can get a good penny for this!"

"It's mine!" cried Maggie, making a lunge for the locket that Daniel held over his head. "Give it to me!"

Daniel swung the chain back and forth, dangerously near the open water. "If we're going to be partners, you can't hold out on me," said Daniel.

"Please give it to me," said Maggie, hopping up to grab the locket that was just beyond her reach. "It was my mother's."

Daniel peered at the tiny gold heart. Then he tried opening it, but it slipped from his greasy fingers back onto the bridge.

This time, Maggie was quick.

"It's mine," she said, snatching up the locket. "You're not to touch it again."

Daniel sniffed. "Well, I guess that means we ain't partners, then. Too bad."

Maggie's head, as usual, filled right up with questions. "Why?"

" 'Cause I know where the treasure is."

"What treasure?"

"You don't know?" he said. "You don't know about the treasure? Where you been livin'? On the moon?" He chuckled at his own joke.

"You don't know about any treasure," said Maggie.

"Oh, no?"

She bit her lip to stop the rest of the questions pushing to come out. Was it in a chest? Were there jewels? Did it come from a pirate ship?

"If you know where there's treasure, why don't you just go and get it?"

"I need help," he said. "I need somebody littler than me."

"Why?"

"Just because," he said. "You with me or not?"

Maggie thought, but not for long. Daniel knew things she didn't, about the city, about where to find food, even if it was out of a garbage can. Maybe he didn't really know where there was treasure, but he knew a lot about how to survive on your own, and she could learn from him.

"Will you help me find Lucky?"

"Sure," he said.

"And will you promise not to hurt him? Ever?"

"Promise cross my heart," he said.

"Then all right," said Maggie. "We're partners."

And they shook on it.

Rats!

The setting sun frowned on Oliver, who was about to dump a garbage can. It was an ordinary tin can, dented and abused like all the others he had seen, with a handle on the lid and two on the side. It reeked with rot.

Why Oliver had chosen this one was anybody's guess. Did his stomach order his feet to stop? Was his better self sleeping on the job? Did he simply forget his manners?

If Bertie could see him now, her eyes would cloud over. She would say, "Oh, Oliver. I am so disappointed in you." And Oliver would slink away, knowing he had let her down.

But Bertie was not here and could not see him. His other self, the one whose job it was to simply be a dog, to romp and play and have a grand old time, stepped up to have a talk with him. "Oliver," it said, "go for it."

Still, Oliver who liked to be clean, who reveled in bubble baths, hesitated.

Clean and hungry or dirty and full? In the end it wasn't so hard to decide.

Oliver sniffed all around the dented can. He pushed a paw against it. He pushed with two paws. Then he took a running start and leapt upon the can, which toppled and rolled and clattered, spewing garbage and one dizzy dog into the street.

Out of a house came a man, flailing his arms and yelling. Oliver scrambled to his feet and dashed away.

Did no one have sympathy for a starving dog?

As the sun disappeared and the great hand of darkness descended, Oliver slunk along in downhearted misery. Was this to be his life now? A life of skulking and begging? Of growing ever more despondent until at last he cared for nothing at all, not even food?

And then, in what he might have called his darkest hour, a light appeared. It shone from a doorway down a narrow alley, between two brick buildings that leaned toward each other whispering secrets.

He stopped and sniffed. The heady smell of cooking food danced toward him, crooked its fingers, and led him in.

Oliver inched through the darkness, keeping low, his eyes and ears and even his tail on full alert.

Stopping in the shadows near the lighted doorway, he watched a man emerge. The man wore a tall white hat, and his white coat was painted with streaks of red and brown. In his hand was a sack that to Oliver smelled delectable. The man carried the sack to the garbage cans lined against the wall like muddied soldiers. Off came the lid of the first can and down went the sack.

The lid closed with a clang.

Oliver waited. He waited until his stomach pinched and howled and demanded immediate action. Then he crept toward the can on feet as light as a cat's. His nose twitched. Even as his brain said "stop!" his stomach urged him on and his mouth watered in readiness.

He had learned one good lesson: if he dumped the can as before, out would come that man to chase him away. What to do? He sniffed the can. He circled it, thinking. Then he stood on his back feet, rested his front paws on the lid, and clamped the handle with his teeth. He gave the handle a tug.

The can rattled, and Oliver scurried back into the shadows.

No one came.

Back he went to try again. This time the lid inched up, the can rattled, but Oliver stayed. *Just a little more, a little more*, his stomach said. Then—*crash!*—over went the can. Oliver sped away.

Out came a different man, who righted the can. With his arms crossed on his dirty white apron, he surveyed the dark alley with narrowed eyes.

"I know you're out there," he said. Reaching into a can, he pulled out a chunk of chewed meat and waved it back and forth. "Hungry?" he said.

Oliver, pulled by his great need, crept toward the meat, ready to grab it and run.

Unless there was more. Unless this man was like his fisherman friend.

"Come on, boy," said the man in a cheery voice. "There's plenty more where this came from."

Oliver made a dash for the meat, but before he could snatch it, the man grabbed Bertie's handkerchief that wasn't Bertie's, and Oliver was caught.

Oliver yelped and cried and snapped his teeth. He wriggled and wiggled and set his haunches down. But he struggled in vain. The man was bigger. The man was determined. He clamped Oliver's snout and dragged him through a puddle toward the lighted door.

"There's no free lunch, my friend," he said. "There's work for you inside." And into a small, cold room went Oliver. The door shut and darkness closed in around him like a fist.

Oliver jumped against the door, whining and crying and begging for release. "AW-OOO! AW-OOO!" he cried, but no one came. When the darkness lifted enough that he could see, he raced around and around the room. He sniffed and scratched and searched for a way out, a hole in the wall, a window, another door, but there was nothing.

At last, exhausted, Oliver lay down upon the cold floor, buried his snout beneath his paw, and cried himself to sleep.

Click. The door opened, and it was the man again. This time he stood with a lantern in his hand, blocking the door. From his other hand dangled something dark and odorous. This he swung gently by its long, skinny tail, back and forth in front of Oliver's nose.

Oliver had seen mice before. He had even driven a few of them crazy, chasing them all over Bertie's house. But he had never seen a rat. This one was sleek and black and big and rotten and dead. Oliver made a dash for the open space between the man's leg and the doorway but was blocked. Then he made another dash for the other side.

The big man stopped him again and again. "No need to run," he said. "You have a job to do. You are our official ratter, my friend."

And with that, he stepped aside.

Oliver was caught by surprise. He was free. He

raced through the doorway and skidded to a stop. Where was he?

Pots hung from a rack over an immense cooking stove. Water drip-drip-dripped into a deep sink. Plates were stacked on open shelves. The faint smell of food lingered in corners and in the air.

Through the kitchen Oliver raced, sliding on the slick floor, into another room. This one had a forest of table legs and chair legs, and Oliver got lost in a maze, looking for a door.

Back he went to the kitchen, sliding to a stop at the man's feet.

The man dangled the dead rat before Oliver again, and Oliver turned away. "Too good for rat, my friend? Such a shame. Our rats are nice and plump from all the food they've stolen. Any one of them would make a fine meal for a dog. Give it a try—that's all I ask." He dropped the rat on the floor.

"All the rats you can eat!" he said. "Not a bad deal. At least you won't be starving in the street."

And with that, he departed the dinner house by the back door, leaving Oliver behind with a rotting dead rat for company.

A Cave in a Forest

"So tell me the truth, partner," said Daniel, pushing his finger into a button on Maggie's coat. "You got no place to go, do you?"

A cold, misty rain had decided to spend the night in the city and was busily chasing everyone inside.

Everyone with an inside place to go.

Maggie looked down at the damp cobblestones. She looked at her wet boots. She slowly shook her head.

"Come with me, then," said Daniel, yanking Maggie by her sleeve.

Maggie pulled her arm free. "Where?"

"My house," said Daniel. "The floor is all you'll get, but it's better than nothing."

"You promised to help find Lucky," said Maggie.

"And I will," said Daniel. "You look on that side of the street, and I'll look on this side. But no dogs in the house. My old man would take a gun to its head."

Maggie's eyes grew round as her buttons. "He would?"

Daniel's laugh had grown rusty with neglect. "Nah! I'm just teasing. If my dad had a gun, he'd shoot himself in the foot with it."

They walked a long way. Maggie's wet boots squished, and her toes had turned to ice. But her stomach was full, and that was a wonderful thing.

No sign of Lucky. Of the dogs they came across, most were wary and desperate, bone thin and covered with mange, but no scruffy brown dog with white-tipped ears and a glimmer of trust still left in his eyes.

Maggie cupped her hands around her mouth and called, "Lucky! Lucky!" But as much as she wanted to find him, she hoped he had found his way home to his owner and the owner of the blue and white hand-kerchief. He was a good-hearted dog. A dog with a good heart deserved a good home.

They entered a neighborhood where the houses were small and ramshackle, gathered close like grumbling old women. No streetlamps lighted their way. A furry something scampered across Maggie's foot, and she jumped back. "What was that?"

Daniel stopped and turned. "What?"

"A cat or something!"

"Not a cat, I wouldn't think," he said. "Cats around here go straight into the stew pot."

"Are you teasing me again?"

"Nope," said Daniel. "Never eat stewed cat before?"

Maggie's stomach lurched. "No!"

"Don't know what you're missing," said Daniel as he continued down the broken slate that served for a walk. He stopped in front of a brick cottage sunk in a sea of weeds with a fence like a row of broken teeth.

"Now you gotta be real quiet," said Daniel. "If my dad is back, he's probably sleeping it off."

"Sleeping it off?"

"The drink," said Daniel. "He does like his drink."

Maggie thought about the drink called sherry that was raised in a toast at Madame's table. It was rose-colored and sipped from delicate crystal glasses. Was this the drink that Daniel's father liked? She followed Daniel through the snow-clotted weeds and around the side of the house.

A door appeared out of nowhere, KEEP OUT scrawled across it in dripping red letters.

"Is your sister here?" whispered Maggie in a shaky voice.

"Nah," said Daniel. "She stays with her friends mostly. Shush, now."

They crept inside. A dim light over the sink showed Maggie what she would rather not have seen: a kitchen the size of Madame Dinglebush's closet, through which every imaginable thing was strewn. Filthy dishes, greasy rags, open cans, food scraps crawling with roaches. A strip of yellow sticky paper covered with flies hung from the ceiling.

If doom had a smell, thought Maggie, it would smell like this.

The sitting room was not much better. Some sort of motor sat squarely in the middle of the floor. A sagging settee and a chair with a broken leg were piled high with yellowed newspapers. The air, what there was of it, carried the odor of clothes worn too long. From an adjacent room came rumbling snores.

"He's sleepin'," Daniel said. "You wait here. I'll bring you a cover."

He came back carrying a blanket full of moth holes. "There you go," he said. "This will keep you warm enough. Be sure to wake early, before my dad."

Maggie sat wrapped inside the woolen blanket, which was itchy and smelled like dirty feet. Despair began its attack, creeping up her legs and into her belly on its way to her heart. She had never in all her ten years felt anything like this monster of despair. It frightened her. It meant to take her over.

Wrapping the blanket more tightly around her, Maggie tried to think what to do. What could one small and not very strong person do to confront a monster of ill intent?

She closed her eyes, which was frightening at first. The blackness looked empty and forbidding. Then her imagination, stronger and far more clever than despair could ever be, began to grow a forest, a leafy green forest, and filled it with singing birds. When Daniel's father's snores invaded her forest, Maggie made a bear's cave. The bear inside made great growling noises in his sleep, but he was a friendly bear known to protect little girls.

She re-counted her many blessings: her warm coat that was only a little bit damp, her boots and stockings and scarf, a friend who knew the ways of the city, a park to sit in, work for which she would soon be paid, her precious locket, a good imagination.

At last Maggie laid down her head, pulled up her knees, and in her cool green forest slid into sleep.

Out of the Bear's Lair

"Get up! Get up! I told you to get up before HIM!"

Half asleep, Maggie rubbed her eyes.

Daniel pulled on her arm. "Get up, I said!"

She heard a huge belch. A man as big as the doorway he stood in surveyed the room with mean little eyes. He wore what Maggie could only guess were underclothes in need of a good scrubbing, and his arms and legs were covered with black fur.

"What have we here, Danny boy?" he said, scratching an armpit. "Guests?" He stepped into the room, and Maggie jumped to her feet.

"Just a pal, Dad," said Daniel, pushing Maggie

behind him. "Never you mind. Me and her is just leaving."

"Not so fast, boy!" The man stalked into the room on his huge, bare feet. "A guest of yours is a guest of mine. Share and share alike, eh?"

"Run!" cried Daniel, giving Maggie a shove. Maggie raced through the kitchen and out the door. Only when she was in the weed patch did she stop and wait for Daniel.

Where was he? She crouched in the weeds and listened. From the house came the sound of Daniel's cries. "Don't! Dad! I won't do it again! Ow! Owww! Stop!"

What should she do? He was in trouble because of her, because he gave her a place to sleep. She ran back through the weeds toward the house as Daniel came racing toward her, nearly knocking her off her feet.

"Go!" he cried. "Run!"

He grabbed her hand and ran for the road, Maggie in flight behind him. They ran and ran until they had no breath left and collapsed at last on a park bench.

Somewhere along the way, Daniel had lost his hat. Sweat rolled down his face. The cheek toward Maggie had a large red welt across it.

"He's a mean man, my dad is," said Daniel, but he said it with some pride.

"I'm sorry," said Maggie.

"Nothin' to be sorry about," said Daniel, puffing himself up.

"But it's all my fault. You let me into your house and—"

Daniel lifted an eyebrow. "Then you owe me one, don'tcha?" he said.

"Oh, yes!" said Maggie. "I do. I most certainly do."

The city was yawning awake. A child cried, a cat whined for its breakfast, the first trolley clanged past. Maggie and Daniel got up from the bench and headed for the factory. "I've got me a good plan," said Daniel. "If it works, we'll be on easy street, the both of us."

"Where's Easy Street?" asked Maggie.

Daniel laughed his rusty laugh. "You don't know nuthin', do ya? Easy Street ain't a real street. It's like . . . a *saying*. If you're livin' on Easy Street, you're livin' high on the hog." He thought for a moment. "That's another way of sayin' the same thing. Stick with me, and I'll teach you all kinds of things. Not fancy things—useful things."

"Tell me your plan," said Maggie as they went up the steps and into the factory. The ladies were settling in, and Speak was stomping through the aisles, scowling.

"Here comes Speak," said Daniel. "I'll tell you later."

Maggie hurried to her table and set to work on the pile of shirt sleeves stacked before her. Perhaps she would be paid today. As the morning wore on, Maggie tried to decide how she would spend her money. First a place to stay, perhaps a small room in the home of a kind lady. What did a room cost? What was the cost of food? Maggie had no idea at all. Perhaps her pay would be enough for everything, or maybe it would buy only an apple and some bread.

The front door opened and closed with a thud. In came two men in top hats and black suits.

Speak came rushing past Maggie's station. He nudged Maggie off her seat and pushed her under the table. Then he made his way toward the two grim-looking men. "May I help you, gentlemen?"

"It's the inspectors," said the old lady to Maggie.

Under the table, Maggie made herself as small as possible. She squeezed herself into a corner. Her heart sent fear flutters into her throat. What would happen now? If the inspectors found her, what would they do? Would she go to jail? Could a child be taken to jail? And last, because she'd had no breakfast, were prisoners fed?

She watched as three pairs of legs came down the aisle toward her station, Mr. Speak stomping on his block and leaning side to side. "Everything's as it should be, gentlemen. We don't break the rules here, no we don't. See how the light comes through these windows. Nothing's too good for our girls."

The inspectors stopped at Daniel's empty station. "And whose work is this?" said one of them.

"Ah, the poor girl took sick. I sent her home, of course."

Where was Daniel? And then Maggie remembered the scrap bin, the one she should be inside right now. But how could she have gotten there, all the way across the room?

Daniel did. He must have. Somehow.

A pair of black-clad legs stopped at her table. A frowning face with glasses pinched to its nose leaned in. "And what have we here? Come out of there, child."

Speak's black eyes shot sparks at Maggie as she crept out and stood before the men. "She's not a child," said Speak. "Tell them how old you are, girl."

How old was she supposed to be? Maggie made a

guess. "Sixteen, sir," she said, making herself as tall as she could.

"Twelve, more like," said the inspector without the glasses.

"Sixteen!" said Speak. "She told me she was sixteen!"

Inspector Glasses gestured with his walking stick. "This is your second violation, Mr. Speak. One more, and you'll be out of here and behind bars."

"Oh, sir," said Speak, clutching his hands together. "No, sir. Please, sir. I run a good operation. This one here"—he pointed at Maggie—"she fooled me. And you know I've got a soft heart for ladies in need."

"Oh, we know you all right, Nicholas Speak. And we'll be keeping a closer eye on you." He turned to Maggie. "And as for you, young lady—"

A wave of dizziness nearly sent Maggie to the floor. "Yes, sir? Am I to go behind bars, sir?"

A corner of the inspector's lip twitched, as if, amazingly, he was about to smile. "You are to leave this place at once, child. And do not turn up at another of these sweatshops. The law was written to protect you. Run along home, now, and tell your parents what happened here today. They could be fined as well for sending you out to work."

"Yes, sir," said Maggie as the inspectors turned to leave, their backs straight as rulers. The door opened and closed with a thump behind them.

Speak grabbed Maggie's arm and shook it hard. "Now you've done it!" he growled.

"But—"

"Get!" he said, and threw Maggie's arm back at her. "You heard the inspectors. Get out of here."

"Yes, sir," said Maggie, putting on her coat. "May I have my pay now, sir?"

Speak's lip curled. "Pay? You get no pay. You ain't old enough to work. Which means you didn't work!"

"But I did!" Tears leapt into Maggie's eyes.

"Give the girl what she's due," said the old lady, without looking up or missing a stitch.

"I'll pay you to keep your mouth shut," said Speak. "Another word and you can leave along with this girl. And that goes for the rest of you."

No one spoke; no one moved.

"Out!" ordered Speak, pointing a straight arm toward the door. "Or do I have to call the cops to come and get you?"

Maggie went up the narrow aisle, tears rolling down her cheeks and off her chin. As she came to the door, Daniel was crawling out of the bin, scraps of cloth clinging to his hair. "Come back tonight," he said. "I'll tell you my plan."

And Maggie, jobless, penniless, but not entirely friendless, went out into the cold.

A Nickel's Worth of Happiness

Maggie lost herself in the streets, going this way and that, left and then right, without a plan. What was she to do now?

Why, look for work of course. The answer was plain as the buttons on her coat. But who would give her employment now? Who would trust in the skills of a ten-going-on-eleven-year-old girl? Mr. Speak was not a good man, but at least he'd given her work.

As her shoulders began to droop, she reminded herself of the many things at which she was proficient: sewing, baking, dusting, scullery scrubbing, hearth sweeping, floor polishing, bug squashing, cat hiding, cartwheeling, dish mending, tree climbing. The list went on and on.

But would anyone hire her for her excellent cartwheels? She thought not.

She would have to sell the locket. What else could she do?

She sat for a time on the steps below a drawing of an immense tooth—J. HAROLD CRUMP, DDS. FINE DENTISTRY. NO PAIN—watching the disorderly life of the city passing in both directions. Automobiles with braying horns careered around clanging trolleys. Loaded-down wagons creaked along as if they had all day to get where they were going. A man in a top hat and tails dashed across the street to meet a lady in a fur coat on the other side. A boy in a flat cap hawked copies of the *Boston Globe*.

She thought about Daniel. She wondered what his plan was and what part she would play in it. She had come to like Daniel. He had given her food and a place to sleep.

But could she trust a person who would harm an animal and think nothing of it?

Maggie got up and found her way at last to the little park where the ducks, unaware of her plight, sailed into their day. She wandered along the paths, looking for Lucky, both sad and happy that he was not there. One of them at least had found that magical place called home.

Would she ever find it again? Had Madame's home ever truly been hers? It was a fine house, as orderly and neat as the bun at the back of Hannah's head, and Maggie wondered why she did not miss it more. She missed Hannah, she missed her little bed, the tree outside her window, the owl, but she missed Madame not one whit.

A home had to be more than bricks piled one upon another and a dust rag in one's hand.

She took out her locket and, opening it, gazed for a long time at the lady she hoped was her mother. The picture was very small, but still Maggie thought she could see in the lady's face the shape of her own. But the eyes were sad eyes, not full of life, as Maggie's still were. How long they would be was the question. Caring for one small person, one self, in the busy greatness of a city was harder than she had ever imagined.

Well, she hadn't imagined it at all. She had taken for granted her place at Hannah's side.

Had Hannah loved her? A little, perhaps more than a little. She had been a kind and patient teacher. But as far back as Maggie could remember, she was never rocked, never hugged, never kissed on the cheek. These quite ordinary things seemed as necessary as food on the table and shelter in the rain, but she did not have them.

She sat on the bench, swinging her legs. Her boots were falling apart, the soles coming loose at the toe. Her stockings were torn, her coat fraying at the cuffs. If she had a mirror, she knew she would find a dirty face in it, and hair like a rat's nest.

When a lady came into the park pushing a pram, Maggie jumped up and asked very politely if the lady might be in need of a nanny. The lady looked horrified, then her face softened. "What is your name, child?" she said.

When Maggie told her, the lady opened her coin purse and offered Maggie a nickel.

Maggie put her hands behind her back. "I would rather work than beg," she said.

"That's very commendable, Maggie," said the lady. "And I'm sure you will find work. But meanwhile, you must eat. You are a growing girl."

Maggie dropped her head. "Yes, ma'am."

The lady laid the nickel on the bench. "Don't be proud, my dear," she said. "Pride never fed an empty stomach." As she walked away, Maggie looked inside the pram. An infant dressed all in pink with a pink face and pink blanket lay like a rosebud waiting to open.

If Maggie had one wish, she would wish that she

could exchange places with that infant. But what a terrible thing to do to an innocent baby. Far better to clutch the precious nickel in her hand and go in search of a meal.

"Thank you!" she cried after the retreating figure of her benefactress. Birds began to sing. Or had she just begun to hear them? Barren trees seemed bright with the promise of leaves. The pond sparkled. The ducks' eyes sparkled. *Everything* sparkled. When the church bells struck the hour and she knew she had nowhere to be, Maggie's heart danced with a fierce feeling of freedom that she had never known.

Off she went at a brisk pace toward the market-place. Automobile horns rang merrily; trolleys were filled with good-hearted, happy people; wagons were pulled by gentle, well-fed horses and driven by fathers who dearly loved their children. The people she passed were smiling, or if not smiling, then only deep in thought. The world blossomed with goodness and hope, and all because of the nickel in her hand.

At the bread shop she bought two buns. The aroma was free. At the apple stand, the seller eyed Maggie suspiciously until Maggie produced a penny for a big, dark red apple. "God bless," said the woman, and that was free as well.

At the cheese stand, she stood staring at a brick

of bright yellow cheddar until the good man behind the counter offered her a thin, small slice for free. It burst in her mouth like sunshine. She bought a penny's worth, tucking it into her pouch along with her buns, the bit of meat from the night before, and the apple. A feast.

She badly needed a comb, but when she found one tossed in a box of assorted barrettes and hair-clips, the price was two cents, a penny more than she had left. While the seller's back was turned, Maggie quickly combed her hair. And that, too, was free.

She left the marketplace with her pouch full, a penny in her pocket, and the feeling that life was a fine thing to have, a gift for which she thanked her mother.

Maggie had no doubt that her mother was no longer alive. She would not have the locket otherwise. A woman desperate enough to leave her infant on a stranger's doorstep would certainly have sold the locket for food.

No, Maggie felt quite certain that whoever had laid her there did so in the hope that Maggie would be well cared for, and only because she herself was dying. She could not bear the thought that the pretty woman in the locket did not love her.

High above the Commons, clouds parted and the

sun appeared as if for the very first time. What snow was left along the walkways began to melt. Beneath the earth crocuses yawned and stretched. A robin's chick came out of its egg and blinked into life; somewhere a baby took its first wobbling steps.

Maggie sat on the edge of a joyful fountain taking a bite of cheese, a bite of bun, and then, sneakily, a bite of apple. It was bad manners not to cut the apple, to eat it in public like a horse, but she had no knife, and the apple, as any good apple will, invited her to just go ahead and eat it.

Never in her life had she had such a happy day, not even on her birthday when Hannah gave her the stockings she had on.

She sat warming herself in the sun, watching children play ring-around-the-rosy while their mothers looked on. When a black dog with yellow eyes came up and sniffed her pouch, she gave him the bit of meat she had saved for Lucky.

Surely, Lucky was home already and had eaten by now.

This Is the End, My Friend

Oliver lay with his snout on his paws, thinking about rats. They were all around him, pushing their ratty little noses into corners, scrabbling their ratty little feet into every nook and cranny of the kitchen. They had come out in twos and threes and then fives and sixes, giving Oliver the once-over and declaring him harmless.

He wasn't exactly happy about being thought harmless, so he got up and growled a couple of times. But even to himself he did not sound convincing, and the rats went about their business.

He was thinking about rats because it was hard

not to think about something that slithered and sniffed around you, that even climbed over you as if you were not there. The thought of eating one sickened him. But he knew that if he didn't, eventually he would die.

How a dog went about dying was a mystery to him. He supposed he could just lie on his side and await the end, so that is what he did. The end went on and on and on, and meanwhile he got so hungry that he began to think that a rat roasted might not be quite as bad as a rat raw.

He fell into a fitful sleep and dreamed about the little girl who called him Lucky. He saw her twirling in the rain, looking up at the sky with her mouth open like a goose and laughing. Then she was running through the rain with her arms wide and he was running behind her, bounding along like a rabbit. He ran so hard that he woke himself up, his four paws scrambling on the floor.

He had chosen the small, dark room to die in. That way he would be no trouble, even to those who gave him the most trouble. When they found him dead, they could shut the door and be done with him. He'd be on his way to Bertie and wouldn't care.

Unless there was one afterlife place for humans and a different one for dogs. But the thought of that just made him more miserable, so he got up and wandered through the kitchen, through the rats, and into the place where the tables were. The rats were happier in the kitchen, if rats could indeed be happy, and so Oliver had the room to himself. He decided to die there instead of in the room with the cold dirt floor. But all he did was fall into a dreamless sleep.

Morning seeped into the room like gray soup. The rats that had fattened themselves on a bag of flour and whatever crumbs they could forage were washing their snouts with their little paws and yawning.

A key turned in the back door lock, and the rats disappeared in a blink of Oliver's eye.

The man had returned. He stood looking down at the flour scattered everywhere and the little paw prints circling through it.

"A fine job you've done," he said, shaking his head at Oliver. "I should give you a good beating for this. But I am a patient man. Unlike my partner, I do not beat dogs or children."

He knelt beside Oliver. He took Oliver's snout into his hand. He made Oliver look into his eyes. "You are a ratter, my friend. Get it into your head. You are a ratter. A ratter chases rats, a ratter kills rats, and a ratter, if he's smart, eats rats."

He shook his finger at Oliver. "Beware of Adolph," he said. "Adolph is *not* a patient man."

Oliver was shooed out of the table room and into the small room, where he spent the longest, most boring day of his life. He almost wished the rats were awake so he could chase a few for fun.

Like most of us, Oliver had a treasure chest of cherished memories that he could open any time he liked. In his grief and misery, he had quite forgotten about it.

He opened it now as he lay on the cold, uncompromising ground, and there they were, spread out before him: choosing his own birthday present at the butcher shop, playing hide-and-seek with a squirrel (the squirrel hid so well that Oliver never found him), getting his back scratched, staying out all night with a passing stray (though he had made Bertie cry), being brushed and brushed and brushed.

He remembered when Bertie had chosen him out of his litter. He remembered the smile on her face when she held him up with his little feet dangling. He remembered the touch of her hand on his head when she said, "Oh, Oliver, you pesky dog."

There were rocks in the box along with the treasure: getting his nose pinched in a mouse trap, being scolded for stealing a ham on Easter Sunday (which he thought now was worth the scolding), watching the wagon that took Bertie away, spending his first night alone.

That evening, the rats' menu changed. Because the flour had been put into a lidded box, the rats chewed their way into a canvas bag of carrots and dumped a tin of sugar onto the floor. After eating all the carrots, they rolled in the sugar and licked each other clean.

They were awful creatures, but they knew how to have a good time. And, really, when you got to know them a little, you could say they weren't unfriendly. They were busy, that's all.

One of them came up to Oliver and, standing on its back feet, tried to converse with him in its ratty language. It seemed to want Oliver to join in the fun, but when he took a lick of sugar, they scurried away screeching.

In came two men, the one Oliver knew and one that he didn't. The one he didn't know had arms and legs like fat sausages and a sour look on his face.

"So *this* is our fine ratter," he said, scowling down at Oliver.

"I thought he might be our ratter, Adolph," said

the other one. "But he isn't. Maybe he's afraid of rats. In any case, he's no good to us. We might as well let him go."

At the word *go*, Oliver's ears perked up.

Adolph rubbed his chin. "There could be some other use for him," he said. "People like their beef, but beef is costly. I say we make a nice dog meat stew. Lots of garlic and spices. They'll never know the difference."

Oliver looked from one face to the other, trying to learn the fate being revealed in words he couldn't understand.

"What did I tell you, my friend?" said the first man, looking down at Oliver with his arms crossed. "You had your chance to guard the food. Now you must be the food."

Taking Oliver by his handkerchief, he dragged him into the small room and closed the door.

"AW-OOOO!" wailed Oliver, in his loudest outburst since the disappearance of Bertie. "AW-OOOO! AW-OOOO!"

Leaping against the door, he cried "AW-OOOO! AW-OOOO!" again and again, while pots clanged and dishes rattled and people cooked and people ate and plates got scraped and the rats stirred in their sleep. "AW-OOOO! AW-OOOO!" howled Oliver.

Even his poor, empty stomach begged for him to stop, but he would not. "AW-OOOO! AW-OOOO! AW-OOOO!" he cried.

A Rat by Any Other Name

From the shadows, Maggie watched as the workers came out of the factory and down the steps. Daniel came last. He looked up the street and down the street.

"Hey, girl!" he said.

Maggie stepped out of the shadows. "My name is Maggie," she said. "You can call me by my name."

"It's good you're here," said Daniel, as if a bird or the wind had spoken and not a living, breathing girl. "I've been working on my plan all day." He pointed to his temple. "In here. It's a wicked good one."

Maggie frowned. "Wicked?"

"Just a sayin'. It's devilish good, is what I mean. A smart plan."

He waited for her to say something. She was always asking questions.

"You can't be a sissy for this plan to work. You gotta be brave."

Biting her tongue, Maggie waited.

"Are you brave, girl?"

"Maggie," she said.

Daniel rolled his eyes. "Are you brave, *Maggie*?"

Maggie considered. Was she brave? She thought she might be. She was learning to be. "Yes," she said.

"And can you keep a secret?"

"Yes," she said.

His eyes lit up as he leaned closer. "We're going after the treasure!"

Maggie's questions began to tumble out, one after another. There was no way to stop them, and out of her mouth they came: Where is it? Is it in a big box? Is there gold? Jewels? Where did it come from? Did it come from a pirate ship?

The more she asked, the more excited she became. Her imagination took flight, swooping her away to a place where reason never lived.

"You'll know soon enough," said Daniel. "But first, supper."

Maggie took out her pouch. "I have some cheese and part of an apple—"

"That ain't supper," said Daniel. "Meat is supper."

So Maggie knew right where they were going. She followed Daniel as before, winding through dark and empty streets, stopping with him at the entrance to the alley.

"This time it's your turn," he said. "I'll keep watch."

They crept down the alley toward the light, staying close to the brick wall. Nearing the door, Maggie began to hear laughter, loud talk, the rattle of dishes, and the cry of a miserable dog. "AW-OOOO! AW-OOOO!"

"That's Lucky!" cried Maggie, as Oliver howled and jumped against the door.

How did Maggie know? She had never heard Oliver cry. And yet she knew the howling dog was the one she called Lucky. For days, he had been running loose around the city. Then he disappeared. If he'd had a home, he'd have gone to it that first night. Lucky wasn't home. He was here.

"Lucky is in there!" she said, pulling on Daniel's sleeve.

"Don't be a goon," he said. "That's just some dog."

"Why would they lock him up?"

"You don't know?"

"No!"

Daniel shook his head and said what he usually said. "You don't know nuthin', do ya? You never ate no dog?"

"No!" cried Maggie, horrified.

"Well, it's not as good as beef," he said with a shrug. "'Less'n it's a pup. But dog and kidney pie? That's the best."

Maggie's stomach recoiled. "We've got to save Lucky," she begged.

Daniel shook his head. "That's not in my plan."

Maggie stood with her chin lifted and her fists on her hips, her blue eyes blazing. "If you won't help Lucky, I won't help you," she said.

Daniel grimaced. "Then I'll get somebody else," he said, but he didn't sound sure of himself.

"Go ahead," she said.

They stood nose to nose, challenging each other to back down. At last Daniel said, "All right, I'll help you get the stupid dog. Then you do everything I say. And no questions."

"It's a deal," said Maggie.

"Here's what we do," said Daniel, hatching another plan on the spot. It took him no time to tell it.

Daniel went to the door, while Maggie waited near it in the shadows.

"Sir?" called Daniel. "Hey, sir!"

A man wearing a tall white hat and an apron streaked with gravy stuck out his head. "What do you want, boy?"

"I found something," said Daniel, crooking his arm. "Out here. I think it's something gold. Or silver. I can't tell in the dark."

"What?" said the man.

"And it's heavy," said Daniel. "Come and look!"

As the man stepped outside, Maggie slipped from the shadows and into the kitchen, past the surprised dishwasher, and straight to the rattling door. She threw it open, and there stood Lucky.

Oliver cocked his head. The girl? He had expected the man. In tail-wagging joy, he nearly knocked her over.

"Run, Lucky!" she cried as she fled across the kitchen, Oliver on her heels. Streaking past Adolph, they ran headlong up the alley.

Maggie could hear Daniel running to catch up, the beat of his boots and a pair of heavier ones, Daniel laughing, a man cursing.

Daniel caught up with Maggie, but Oliver, faster than both, had gone out of sight. They ran and ran until they could run no more. Adolph, who was fat and slow, had lost them.

"So much for supper!" said Daniel, when he had gotten his breath back.

Maggie dug into her pouch. "Here," she said as she offered Daniel a bit of cheese.

"Keep it," he said. "We've got work to do." He looked around. "Where is that stupid dog of yours, anyway? He didn't even stick around long enough to thank us."

"Lucky!" Maggie called.

Oliver wriggled out from under an automobile, wagging his tail. His nose was covered with grease.

"Lucky!" Maggie cried. "Come here."

Oliver gave the boy a wide berth, but he let the girl hug and kiss him much the way Bertie did, as if she might never stop.

"The dog can't come with us," said Daniel.

Maggie looked up, dog slobber shining on her cheeks. "Why not?"

"Because he's a *dog*! Dogs make noise." Daniel shook his head in disgust. "Remember the deal. I call the shots. You keep your mouth shut."

Maggie stood. She looked down at Lucky, whose tail sailed back and forth like a conductor's baton. "He'll be good," she said. "Why can't he come?"

"I said, no questions! You ask too many questions for a girl."

Maggie frowned. Is that why Hannah had stopped her from asking her many questions? Because she was a girl? Were girls not supposed to have questions?

Her frown deepened. That couldn't be right. If birds weren't supposed to sing, they wouldn't sing. If dogs were not meant to bark, they wouldn't bark. If girls weren't supposed to have questions, they wouldn't have them.

"And you don't ask enough questions," said Maggie. "You do things without thinking. You jump without knowing how deep the water is."

"What water? What are you talking about?"

"It's a saying," said Maggie, who wasn't sure that it was.

"I make plans," said Daniel. "How do you think I make plans?" He poked his head. "I use my brain. I think. And I'm thinking this dog can't come."

Oliver—whose one thought was "where's the food?"—stood waiting for the endless talk to end.

Maggie gave in. "You can't come, Lucky," she said, scratching Oliver's chin. "Lie down and wait here. I'll be back for you." She patted the sidewalk, but Oliver just kept wagging his tail, and when she began to walk away with the boy, he followed.

The boy turned an angry face. "Get!" he said,

stomping his foot. Oliver skipped away and stopped. The boy bent and picked up a rock.

The girl grabbed his arm. "No!" she cried.

Oliver ran. When he came to the end of the street, he turned and looked back. He wanted to follow the girl who had saved him, but he was afraid of the boy. Chewing on that dilemma like a bone, Oliver decided to follow the girl at a distance, keeping his eye on the boy.

He knew a rat when he saw one.

A Wink of Gold

"Aw, I wasn't going to throw it," said Daniel. "I was just scarin' him, that's all. He was going to ruin the plan!"

Maggie walked with her head down and her hands pushed into her pockets. "I don't think you have a plan. And I don't think there's a real treasure, either."

Mist from the harbor reached into the city and settled like snow.

"There is a treasure," said Daniel. "And it's gold."

"Then why don't you have it already?"

"Because," said Daniel.

"Because why?"

"Because," he said, "there has to be somebody as small as you. That's part of the plan."

"Then tell me where it is and how you came to know about it."

They made their way through the fog, two small figures with hollow stomachs wrapped in threadbare clothes. Daniel's face was screwed up in thought. "My dad said not to tell anybody," he said.

"Your dad? What's your dad got to do with it?" Just the thought of the big, scary bear made Maggie's skin crawl.

"It's where he used to work. At this rich lady's house."

"Then why didn't he get it?"

"I told you!" said Daniel in disgust. "It's got to be somebody small. Somebody small and quick. And it has to be done at night."

Maggie stopped. "You didn't say we had to steal!" she said. "I'm not a thief."

"Did I say steal?" said Daniel. "Did I?"

"No, but—"

"Do you want to see it?"

She planted her feet. "I don't know."

"Suit yourself," he said. "I seen it once. It's the most beeyootiful thing. All made of gold."

She crossed her arms. "*What's* made of gold? What is it?"

"You'll see," he said. "Come on."

Why did Maggie follow Daniel? For one thing, she had nowhere else to go. She was cold and hungry, all alone, and not yet eleven. She stopped asking all the questions that might have made her turn back, back to where Oliver waited.

A skinny black cat came out of the shadows and threaded through her ankles. "All right," she said at last. "But just to look."

A coach-and-four came clattering through the fog, a black shape drawn by four sleek black horses. A pair of bright blue eyes peered out through gray mist. "It's the duchess!" cried Maggie. "Look! Daniel! It's the Duchess of Landsaway's coach."

But Daniel barely glanced up. "I seen it before," he said.

At last, they came up out of the fog and entered a place that even Maggie with her bursting imagination could never have dreamed of, a kingdom of stately homes, far grander than any she had ever seen. They were done up like frosted layer cakes, with gatehouses and turrets and long, curving drives. Some sat smugly behind tall iron fences. Some had sweeping lawns and gardens that seemed to invite the passerby in, but their doors, like all the others, were forbidding.

At last they came to the grandest of all. Surrounded by trees, it sat on a little rise above the other homes, its marble walls gleaming in the moonlight.

Maggie stared with her mouth open. Was she dreaming? Was it a real home with real people living inside? Did they get lost in there? How did they find their bedrooms?

"The lights are still on," said Daniel. "Keep in the trees and don't say a word."

Maggie's heart was an anxious bird beating its wings in her throat. She crept through the trees behind Daniel, keeping low, her curiosity drawing her along. When a twig broke beneath her boot, she jumped. Daniel turned with his finger to his lips. "Shhh!"

Daniel stopped where the wood ended and the lawn began. "There!" he said, pointing toward the house.

"Where?" said Maggie.

On the lower story, a light went out.

"It was right there," Daniel said, jabbing his finger toward a darkened window. "Did you see it?"

Maggie, who thought she might have gotten the quickest glimpse of something shining, now doubted her eyes. "No," she said.

A cracking sound and then another made them turn. Something was bounding toward them through the woods. "Lucky!" cried Maggie as the shaggy, smelly dog leapt against her, licking her face.

"Not the dog!" said Daniel.

Maggie hugged and patted Lucky while Daniel watched with a sour look on his face.

"Look, Lucky!" she said. "Isn't this the finest house you've ever seen?"

But Oliver only had eyes for Maggie.

"Come on," said Daniel. "It's all ruined now. Let's get out of here."

Maggie and Daniel crept back through the wood while Oliver ran in circles, sniffing every tree, every hole in the ground, every place an animal might have been. He was delirious with freedom.

But when they reached the street, he stayed a good ways behind. He had taken a chance running up to the girl and been rewarded for it, but now he became cautious again. The boy could not be trusted.

"Come on, Lucky!" the girl cried, but when he did not go to her, she gave up and went along with the boy.

Oliver sniffed the gutters in search of anything edible. Anything except a rat. But the gutters had been swept clean and washed down. This place was the worst sort of place for a dog because it had no smell.

He loped along, stopping to sniff, then loping some more to catch up with the girl. She and the boy had gone into a very different kind of place, a place of small houses and dark streets and a far better place for Oliver. There were animal droppings and enticing bits of garbage tossed about. He was sniffing along a wooden fence when he smelled something that made him lift his head and sniff the air.

Smoke.

He went back to his business until the smoke got in his way again.

He barked. Up the street toward where a thousand tongues of orange flame stretched and snapped against the dark night sky.

A Daring Rescue

"It's my house!" cried Daniel. He raced toward the fire yelling, "Dad! Dad!" and Maggie stayed with him, Oliver not far behind.

They stopped at the broken fence, their eyes wide, as fire licked up the side of the house, reaching for the roof.

Daniel yelled for his father again. "I've got to get him out," he said when no answer came, and he dashed into the weeds.

"No! Daniel!" cried Maggie. "You can't go in there!"

Oliver began to bark, sharp loud barks meant to

alert the neighbors. A few people had come out of their houses and were gathering in the street.

Maggie darted into the weeds, calling Daniel's name. Oliver bounded after her. When they came to the door, Daniel threw it open. Clouds of black smoke billowed out. He went through it, choking and calling for his father.

Maggie, more frightened than she had ever been in her life, hung back. But when Lucky went past her into the house, she followed him. If Daniel's father was in the bedroom where the fire was, they had to save him.

The kitchen was thick with smoke. Maggie tied her scarf around her nose and mouth, and dropping to her hands and knees where the air was clearer, she crawled across the kitchen floor. The fire cracked and hissed and spat. She could hear Daniel crying, "Dad! Get up, Dad! There's a fire! Wake up! Dad!"

In the bedroom, where Maggie could hardly see for all the smoke, Daniel, coughing and crying, was pulling on his father's arm. But his father, a great lump upon a mattress, wasn't moving.

Maggie grabbed the man's hairy ankle and pulled. Choking on the smoke and pulling as hard as they could, Maggie and Daniel got the big lump to the edge of the mattress. He toppled over and landed with a thump on the floor.

"Wha . . . ?" he said. Rolling over, he began to snore.

Fire was snaking its way across the wall. "Get up, Dad!" cried Daniel.

Oliver didn't like the looks of this one bit. He latched onto the girl's coat, but she would not let go of the big man's leg. She was crying and pulling, and her face was bright red. She and the boy could budge the great weight of the man only a little. So Oliver latched onto the big man's nightshirt instead of the coat and started yanking.

The man began to slide across the floor. It was hard going. The boy and girl, each with an arm, grunted and pulled. Oliver yanked, set his feet, and yanked some more. The fire popped and cracked. Across the kitchen floor slid the man, inch by inch, then through the door and down the steps, where he toppled over and landed in the yard.

"Wha . . . ?" he said, and sat up, rubbing his head. Then he lay back down with a smile on his face and went back to sleep.

From several blocks away came the *clang-clang-clang* of a fire bell, pounding hooves, and the hiss of steam. A fire engine was on its way. Daniel knelt by his father's side while his father slept, and at last the firemen came. Lifting Daniel's father under the arms, they dragged him out to the street.

One fireman stayed with Maggie, Daniel, and

Oliver, hurrying them along. "How did you manage to pull him out here?" said the fireman when they got to the street. "The man weighs a half ton!"

"Lucky helped," said Maggie. Oliver was panting, his tongue hanging out of his mouth. "Lucky's a hero," she said.

"Woof!" said Oliver, which only meant he was ready to get out of there, but they all laughed, even Daniel.

"You two got somebody to stay with?" asked the fireman.

Daniel nodded solemnly. "Our sister," he said.

"You can visit your father in the hospital in the morning," said the fireman.

The two other firemen were holding on to a huge, heavy hose, training water on the burning house, but the fire was quickly claiming it. All they could do was work to save the houses on either side. The three horses whose job it was to haul the big steam engine waited in the street. They were proud horses, chosen out of hundreds of their kind for their strength and patience.

"There goes my house," said Daniel. "Now there isn't even a floor to sleep on." His face was covered with soot, through which his tears made crooked tracks.

·Where To?

Maggie and Daniel leaned into the pond, washing the soot from their faces and hands.

"It's freezin' cold!" cried Daniel, wiping his face with a sooty sleeve.

"It's not so bad," said Maggie. "Lucky likes it."

Oliver had leapt right into the water and was splashing through the broken ice like a puppy.

Except for a ragged man sleeping on a bench, the Common was empty of people. Now the creatures of night reigned. An opossum peered out from her den. A raccoon chattered. Moths flitted past. Trees lifted their bare limbs to the night sky and tried to touch the stars.

Oliver jumped out of the pond and shook himself all over. He was cold. Cold and wet and tired and, more than anything, hungry. It was past time to begin his search for supper, but the girl's hand lay on his back. Her coat held the memory of fire, but it warmed his side. He wished for another kind of fire, like the fire at Bertie's, where he and the girl could lie down on the hearth and warm themselves until morning.

Maggie was remembering all the warm places she had ever been, which were mostly at Madame's. She had been warm once inside her mother, but she could not remember that. Had she been warm in her basket on Madame's stoop? Had she been found in winter or in summer when a blanket might not have been needed?

Why had she not asked Hannah that question when she had asked so many others?

Did Hannah ever think of her? Did Hannah miss her?

Daniel sat on the edge of the pond, wrapped in his arms and shivering. "It's time I stowed away," he said.

"To Australia?" said Maggie. "What if it's just as cold there?"

Lucky was sniffing at her pocket.

"Can't be," said Daniel. "No place is as cold as Boston."

"Maybe I'll go, too," said Maggie.

Daniel scoffed. "A girl can't be a stowaway."

"Why not?"

"Well, because," said Daniel.

"Because why?"

He frowned. "It ain't right."

"That's no answer," said Maggie. "What's a stow-away, anyway?"

Daniel rolled his eyes. "Don't you know nuthin'? It's a person who stows away. He hides on the boat until it's out to sea and it's too late to put him off."

"I can hide as well as you," said Maggie.

"You're a girl," said Daniel, as if that were a good answer.

"I don't think Lucky would come," she said.

Oliver's nose was almost inside her pocket.

"I'm hungry," said Daniel.

"We can't go to the place where they captured Lucky," said Maggie.

"No," said Daniel. "We can't go there." And Maggie could tell that Daniel had changed his mind about Lucky because Lucky had helped save his father.

"If we had that clock," said Daniel, "we could sell it and have a real dinner in a real dinner house."

"Clock? What clock?"

"The gold one. The one in the window."

Maggie's eyebrows went up. "It was a clock? The treasure is only a clock?"

"Not *only* a clock," he said. "It's the most beeyoo-tiful clock in the whole wide world. There's a ruby right on the top as big as my fist." He made a fist to show her. "And angels made of gold flying all around. And diamonds, too, right there in the numbers."

The picture Daniel painted set itself in Maggie's mind. Of all the treasures in Madame's house, none were as fabulous as the clock Daniel described.

"Too bad you didn't see it," he said. "If you did, you would never, ever forget it."

"We could see it in the daytime," said Maggie.

"Nah," he said. "Too risky."

"Why? We're only going to look."

Daniel frowned. "I guess we could go real early in the morning."

"Let's!" said Maggie, her curiosity stronger even than hunger.

Lucky had gotten hold of her pouch and was pulling it out of her pocket.

"My bun!" Maggie cried. She opened her pouch and tore the bun into three equal pieces.

"What else you got in there?" said Daniel,

grabbing her pouch. He reached inside and pulled out a penny.

"You're holding out on me!" he said.

"I forgot," said Maggie, surprised that she could forget she had a whole penny left from the nickel she'd been given.

Daniel pocketed the penny and went back inside the pouch. Out came a shriveled apple core, which he tossed. Last came the locket. "We're going to have to sell this," he said, swinging the tiny spark of light.

"*We* are not," said Maggie, snatching back the locket. "And *I* am not. Not ever!" She put the locket back inside her pouch and pushed the pouch deep into her pocket.

They left the Common and wandered the streets looking for shelter. At last all three settled in the shadows of a boarded-over doorway set back off the street. One stomach rumbled, then another, then a third, until at last they fell asleep.

Tick Tock, It's Not Your Clock

Dawn came creeping up the sky. A mockingbird launched into one of the songs from its repertoire. Maggie sat and stretched. She poked Daniel's shoulder. "Wake up."

"Hmmmph," said Daniel.

Oliver opened one eye and closed it again.

"Let's go see the clock," said Maggie. Her mind had been so fixed on the golden clock that she had dreamed about it.

Daniel sat up rubbing his eyes. "I got to go to work," he said. "Speak's paying us today."

"There's time," said Maggie.

Daniel got to his feet. "All right," he said. "But remember, I'm the one in charge."

"In charge of what?"

"In charge of us," he said.

The city lay slumbering as Maggie, Daniel, and Oliver made their way through damp streets gleaming pink and gold in the morning light. Their breath sent clouds into the clear, cold air.

"I sure hope my dad's all fixed. He won't stay in a hospital, I know that," said Daniel. "He's at his pub, I'll bet."

"Maybe he went to work."

Daniel shook his head. "Nah. The lady gave him the sack."

"What for?"

Daniel shrugged. "Stole something, most likely. That's how he is."

"It's not how you have to be," said Maggie.

"I s'pose not," said Daniel. "It's just what I learnt, is all."

They made their way through the kingdom of stately homes and went up through the trees again.

"Quiet, Lucky," said Daniel, even though Oliver had been exactly that.

The sun rose, turning the white mansion the color of a ripe peach. As they stood watching, something in a downstairs window began to glow and sparkle, and Maggie could see as plain as the morning that it was the clock. "Oh!" she said.

"Didn't I tell ya?" said Daniel. "Isn't it the most beeyootiful thing you ever seen?"

"Oh, yes!" said Maggie.

"There's diamonds, just like I said, and emeralds on the feet," he said.

"Where?" said Maggie. "I can't see any feet. And where are the angels and the big ruby?"

Daniel took her hand. "Come on," he said. Crouching, he made his way across the lawn with Maggie creeping along behind him.

Oliver, not knowing what the fuss was all about, waited where he was. He watched the boy and girl stare at the shiny thing in the window. He watched the boy tugging at a window. He saw the window slide up just a little ways. He saw the boy point to the window and the girl shake her head.

Now the girl was pulling on the boy's arm. Oliver yipped for the girl to come. When the girl looked back, the boy grabbed her pouch and took the shiny golden thing out of it. Then the golden thing went sailing over their heads and straight through the open window.

Caught!

"My locket!" cried Maggie. "Why did you do that?"

"It slipped out of my hand!" said Daniel with a wicked little smile.

Tears flooded Maggie's eyes. "It didn't slip! You threw it! I saw you!"

"Hush!" he said. "The lady will hear you."

"Get my locket," said Maggie. She stamped her foot. "Get my locket *now*."

"Can't," said Daniel, shrugging. "I can't fit through the window."

Maggie glowered. "This was your plan all along, wasn't it?"

Daniel grinned. "You gotta admit, it's a good one!"

"You are a mean, nasty scoundrel," she said. "That's what I know."

"You'd better get your locket before the lady wakes up," he said.

Maggie tried to think of another way to get her locket back. She could knock on the door and ask for it, but how to explain how it got there in the first place? She looked up at the window. In a flash, she could be in and out with her locket.

"Give me a boost," she said at last.

"Now you're gettin' smart," said Daniel. He made a step with his hands. "Pass me down the clock first. But be real careful with it."

"I'm not getting the clock," said Maggie in a hoarse whisper. "I'm getting my locket."

"You have to do what I say," said Daniel. "I'm the boss!"

Oliver whined and leapt against the house.

"Quiet, Lucky!" said Daniel.

Maggie shinnied over the sill and into the house. Her eyes darted around the room, with its fancy drapes and satin furnishings. In her haste to get inside, she had barely glanced at the golden clock. Her locket was the real treasure.

But where was it?

She crawled over the carpet, peering beneath sofas with fringe and chairs with feet like a hawk's claws. She made her way to a second sofa and finally a third. She lifted the fringe, and there it was. Slipping her hand under the sofa, she snatched her locket.

A light came on. Maggie froze. A woman said in a sharp, no-nonsense voice, "Is there someone in here?"

Maggie, breathless with fear, scooted under the sofa. From there she watched a pair of sturdy black shoes cross the carpet. She heard the window close and the latch click. The black shoes went past her again, and the light went out.

With a pounding heart, Maggie slid out from under the sofa, ran to the window, and pulled up the latch. She was about to push the window open when the light came on again.

"Stop where you are!" rang the woman's voice.

Maggie whipped around. There stood the owner of the black shoes, a tall, bony woman with a knife-sharp nose and eyes as black as pitch.

Beside her, in a dress of the palest blue silk, stood the little duchess.

The Lady in the Locket

The tall, thin woman had Maggie by the arm. "What have you taken?" she said, her black eyes boring into Maggie's.

"Nothing! Honest!" cried Maggie, trying to break free.

The woman shook Maggie until her teeth rattled. "Tell me the truth, child!"

"Release the girl, Bridget," said the duchess very quietly.

Bridget's black eyes snapped. With a last shake, she released Maggie, who fell back, faint with fear and hunger.

The duchess held out her small hand. "Come, child," she said. "Come and sit. Bring the child a cup of water, Bridget," she said.

"But, ma'am," said Bridget.

"Do as I say," said the duchess firmly, and Bridget stomped out of the room.

"Now, tell me," said the duchess when they were seated on a yellow silk sofa. "What mischief were you up to?" She clasped her hands and waited for Maggie's explanation.

"I wasn't going to steal the clock," said Maggie, who sat on the edge of the sofa with her back straight as a washboard. "I wouldn't steal!"

"The clock?" said the duchess. "The clock by the window?" She turned to look at it. "It's very valuable," she said.

"I wasn't going to take it," said Maggie, with tear-filled eyes and a trembling lip.

"I shouldn't think so," said the duchess. "It wouldn't be a very nice thing to do."

Bridget came back with a cup of water and set it on a little table next to Maggie. "Ask what she's got in her hand," said Bridget.

The duchess looked suddenly very sad. At last she said, "What is your name, child?"

With a lowered chin and downcast eyes, Maggie muttered her name.

"Have you stolen something from me, Maggie?" the duchess said. "You can tell me. No one is going to hurt you."

"It's mine," cried Maggie. She clutched the locket to her chest.

"May I see it?" said the duchess.

Maggie opened her hand. The tiny heart and its chain lay on her dirty palm.

The duchess's blue eyes grew wide. She lifted the heart by its delicate chain. "Why, this is Ada's locket!" she gasped. "Wherever did you get it?"

"It was given to me," said Maggie, which was the simple truth and all she knew.

"There's a dog outside," said Bridget from across the room. "A stray. He's barking."

"That's Lucky," said Maggie. "He's my dog. He won't hurt anybody."

"Shall I call someone to take him away?" said Bridget.

"No!" cried Maggie.

"Let him in," said the duchess.

"But, ma'am!"

"Bridget," said the duchess, "I asked you to let him in. Now you may go and fetch him yourself."

Bridget huffed out of the room, skirts flying.

"Maggie," said the duchess, "you must tell me where this locket came from. It's very important."

"I would tell you if I could," said Maggie. "All I know is what Hannah told me."

Like a bird with a bright idea, the duchess cocked her head. "Now I remember you!" she said. "You work for Louisa Dinglebush. I thought I remembered those bright blue eyes. What are you doing so far from home?"

"Madame dismissed me," said Maggie.

The duchess frowned. "Did you steal from her?"

"No!" cried Maggie. "I would never!"

"Then why, child?" said the duchess. "Tell me the truth, now."

"I spoke to you," said Maggie.

"Oh, dear!" said the duchess. "She dismissed you for that? Then it's all my fault."

"No, ma'am," said Maggie. "It was no one's fault."

The duchess gazed down at the locket in her hand. "Tell me about this trinket, Maggie," she said. "Tell me all you know."

So Maggie told her what she knew, which wasn't much. "I think this locket belonged to whoever left me there," said Maggie. "Because Hannah had put it in my pouch before she sent me out."

"Into the cold," said the duchess, shaking her head.

"It wasn't too awfully cold," said Maggie. "And I had my warm coat."

The duchess, with tears in her eyes, opened the tiny locket. "Ada," she whispered.

"You know that lady?" said Maggie.

"She was my daughter," said the duchess. "Ada McGinnis." She raised her eyes to Maggie. "And you, my child, I believe you are my own dear grandchild."

Maggie was dumbfounded. The duchess's granddaughter? All her life she had been Maggie McGinnis and never known it? What an impossibly wonderful thing!

Oliver came bounding into the room. He laid his snout in Maggie's lap and beat his tail for all he was worth. When the boy had taken off, disappearing into the trees, Oliver had waited beneath the window for Maggie to come out. When she didn't come, he began to be afraid that he would never see her again. But here she was with a lady who smelled like Bertie.

Bridget stood stiffly at the duchess's side. "The dog smells foul," she said.

"Then give him a bath," said the duchess. "A bath and a good meaty bone. His ribs are showing through."

She smiled fondly at Maggie. "And shall you have a bath and a good meal, too, my dear?"

"Oh, yes! Please!" said Maggie.

Magic

Maggie lay in water up to her chin, soaking in bubbles. She had never in her life had a bubble bath, although it was rumored that Madame took them all the time. The bubbles made her sneeze, but she didn't mind. The water was deliciously warm.

She was trying not to think about Daniel, but the more she tried, the more he pushed into her mind. She was furious with him. He had played the meanest trick ever.

Still, she wondered where he was and if he'd found a place to sleep and some supper. His life had been far harder than hers. His father was cruel and had taught him all the wrong lessons. Daniel survived as best he could, and not always honestly.

Would she have come to that in the end? If the duchess had not claimed her—the duchess, her *grandmother*—what would have become of her?

Maggie still could not believe her good fortune. She had pinched herself several times already to make sure she wasn't dreaming.

Had a guardian angel been watching over her? Leading her by this crooked path in its own good time? Why had her angel waited until now? Was she meant to learn something about being a better person? Already she was as good as she knew how to be.

Maggie climbed out of the deep tub, the kind of tub that before this day she had only scrubbed. She wrapped herself in a thick, warm towel. In the mirror over the sink, she looked at her face, which was clean and rosy. She took a comb from the shelf and pulled it through her wet curls.

"Are you Maggie?" she asked the image in the mirror. "Is this real?"

There came a knock on the door, and Maggie went to open it.

"Here are some clothes that belonged to your mother," said the duchess. "They're a bit old-fashioned, but I thought you might like them."

Maggie took the soft clothes and shoes into her arms. "Oh, yes!" she said, which was fast becoming her answer to everything.

"Your dog—"

"Lucky," said Maggie.

"Yes, Lucky," said the duchess. "He's had his bath. And do you know, his handkerchief is one I lost while waving out the window of my coach!"

"Grandmother?"

"Yes, child?"

"Do you think there's such a thing as magic?"

"Why, of course there is," said the duchess. "Yesterday I had no little girl to spoil and love, and today I have you. If that isn't magic, I don't know what is."

Maggie held the dark blue velvet dress before her. She tried to imagine her mother as a girl her age wearing this dress. Was she a happy girl? Did she laugh and play and never know the sharp teeth of hunger or the pain of unhappiness?

That could not be. She had lost her mother, after all. Or her mother lost her, a terrible, painful thing. How could that happen? Perhaps tonight, if she asked, her grandmother would tell her what Hannah didn't know.

Maggie slipped on slithery silk stockings she had

never seen the likes of and the velvet dress with its thirty tiny buttons. The black shoes were too big, but she wore them anyway. She peered into the mirror. "Maggie McGinnis," she said to her new self. "Hello, Maggie McGinnis." She decided to say her name every day at least a hundred times until it became realer than real.

"Don't you look lovely!" said the duchess when Maggie opened the door and went out into the hall.

"I think I must!" said Maggie, smiling as she had never smiled before. She took her grandmother's hand and stepped like magic into another life.

Oliver could not get over the fresh, clean smell of himself. What a handsome coat he had when it was washed and brushed! The woman called Cook had been rough with him at first. She had yanked him harshly and stolen his handkerchief. But the bath she'd drawn in the washtub was just the way he liked it, warm and full of bubbles.

He liked the way she smelled. Not of bread and applesauce like Bertie. Cook smelled meaty. All the while she scrubbed Oliver, he sniffed her neck, her arm, her ear. After a while, she began to laugh. "Oh, you're a pesky one, you are," she said. And Oliver began to love her.

He wondered if he might be allowed to stay. He

wondered where the girl was. He wondered if he might be given a second meaty bone. He wondered if this house had any rats living in it. He hoped not.

"Lucky!"

Was that the girl? The one called Maggie? She didn't look the same. Her face was clean. She smelled like soap. But she scratched Oliver under the chin just like the other Maggie did.

He licked her hand. Except for the soap, she smelled and tasted the same.

"Guess what?" she said. "You're to have a nice

little bed right next to mine. Your very own bed. Come on, I'll show you."

Oliver followed Maggie up a flight of curving stairs, down a long hallway, and into a room that was the size of Bertie's house. He did the thing that always made Bertie so mad. He leapt up on the bed. Turning three times, he settled in.

"Lucky!" cried Maggie. "You can't sleep in that bed. It's my bed. Your bed is—"

But Oliver, who had had enough adventure to last a lifetime, had fallen fast asleep.

March 12, 1905

D*ear Hannah,*
        I hope this letter finds you well. As for me,
     I am very well. I believe you will be—

"Grandmother?"

"Yes?"

"How do you spell *surprised*?"

     surprised to learn that I am now living at the
     home of my grandmother, the Duchess of—

"Grandmother?"

"Yes, child?"

"Will you spell what you are the duchess of?"

"L-A-N-D-S-A-W-A-Y. Landsaway. I made it up, you know."

"You did?"

"Oh, yes," said her grandmother with a merry little chuckle. "I thought Boston needed a duchess, and so I decided to become one."

"I think I shall be a duchess, too," said Maggie. "How do you spell *residing*?"

Her grandmother spelled the word and Maggie changed *living* to *residing* because it made her letter sound far more important.

> *It is a fine home, and I sleep upon silk sheets.*
> *Lucky—*

She stopped and laid down her pen. Hannah didn't know about Lucky. She knew nothing of the dire events that befell Maggie after her dismissal. But Maggie could not tell Hannah everything. Her letter would be far too long, and her hand, already cramped, would probably fall off. She took up the pen and crossed out her last sentence.

Still, it was far better than a visit and the chance of seeing Madame again.

> *The story of my coming into this world has*
> *a sad begin—*

"Grandmother?"

"Yes, child?"

"How many *n*'s has the word *beginning*?"

"I believe it has three," said the duchess, "but not all in a row."

> *—ning. My mother took up with a footman. My grandfather dismissed the footman and sent my mother away. Then my grandmother sent my grandfather away. Grandmother searched and searched for her daughter. All she came to know was that my mother had died and was buried in an unmarked grave.*

"Grandmother?"

"Yes, child?"

"Why didn't my mother give me to you?"

The duchess sighed. "I believe Ada was trying to do just that," she said. "The morning you were found, a woman was struck and killed by an automobile. The story was in the *Globe*. After the accident, a woman of means found the child on her doorstep and offered to take her in."

"Madame Dinglebush!" said Maggie.

"The dead woman was never identified. I never thought for a moment that she could be my Ada."

"I'm sorry, Grandmother," said Maggie. "I ask too many questions, don't I?"

"Of course not!" said the duchess. "One can never ask too many questions. It's how one learns. One would be quite stupid otherwise. Go on with your letter, my dear."

With many stops and starts, and many questions about how to say what she wished to say, only fancier, Maggie continued.

> *When Grandmother saw my locket, she knew at once that I was her granddaughter. I tremble to think what might have happened had you not slipped it into my little pouch. I am most grateful to you for that. You watched over me and taught me how to be a good person, and for that I am grateful as well. When I count my many blessings, I will always count you.*

> *Your friend,*
> *Maggie McGinnis*
> *Second Duchess of Landsaway*

QUESTIONS FOR THE AUTHOR

VALERIE HOBBS

What did you want to be when you grew up?
More than anything, I wanted to be a professional ice-skater.

When did you realize you wanted to be a writer?
There wasn't any one moment of realization. It just came over me sneakily, and then I realized that I was one.

What's your first childhood memory?
Sticking my finger into an open light socket. It was almost my last memory!

What's your most embarrassing childhood memory?
Running naked out of the bathroom when the lights went off into the living room full of people. Of course, the lights came right back on and there I was.

What's your favorite childhood memory?
Christmas morning, deep snow, a "real" baby carriage and doll, a miniature piano.

As a young person, who did you look up to most?
Lad from *Lad, A Dog,* by Albert Payson Terhune. I'm serious.

What was your worst subject in school?
Math.

What was your best subject in school?
English.

What was your first job?
Selling ladies' underwear at Woolworth's.

How did you celebrate publishing your first book?
I took myself to lunch at an expensive restaurant downtown and had a glass of wine. Then I wrote notes for my next book all over the paper table cover. But I didn't write the book.

Where do you write your books?
In my "office" upstairs, which is also the TV room.

Where do you find inspiration for your writing?
Walking in Elings Park which has an ocean view and hang gliders.

Which of your characters is most like you?
They all are in some way, but Bronwyn Lewis is the most me.

When you finish a book, who reads it first?
My husband, Jack.

Are you a morning person or a night owl?
Definitely, morning.

What's your idea of the best meal ever?
Fresh-caught salmon from the Pacific Northwest, a glass of
Jaffurs Syrah, and chocolate mousse for dessert.

Which do you like better: cats or dogs?
Dogs (but please don't tell Molly, my cat).

What do you value most in your friends?
Their ability to listen and to love me unconditionally.

Where do you go for peace and quiet?
My backyard.

What makes you laugh out loud?
My grandkids, Diego (six) and Rafael (two and a half). Just about
everything they do cracks me up.

What's your favorite song?
"I Will Survive."

Who is your favorite fictional character?
Dorothea Brooke, *Middlemarch*.

What are you most afraid of?
Poverty.

What time of the year do you like best?
Fall (with spring a close second).

What is your favorite TV show?
The Office.

If you were stranded on a desert island, who would you want for company?
My husband, Jack.

If you could travel in time, where would you go?
Paris, 1920.

What's the best advice you have ever received about writing?
Write from the heart.

What do you want readers to remember about your books?
We are amazing and powerful human beings, each and every one of us. Sometimes we lose our way but we can always find it again.

What would you do if you ever stopped writing?
Read. Travel. Whine a lot.

What do you like best about yourself?
My sense of humor.

What is your worst habit?
I fall into pessimism and believe that I will never write another book, or a good enough book.

What do you consider to be your greatest accomplishment?
Learning little by little to see the bright side of things.

Where in the world do you feel most at home?
Santa Barbara, California, and Volcano, Hawaii.

What do you wish you could do better?
I wish I could write and illustrate a picture book.

What would your readers be most surprised to learn about you?
I once raced cars.

QUESTIONS FOR THE ILLUSTRATOR

JENNIFER THERMES

What did you want to be when you grew up?
At different times in my life I wanted to be a jockey (before I realized I was too tall), a ballerina, a farmer, and a veterinarian.

When did you realize you wanted to be an illustrator?
Though I'd been drawing my whole life, it didn't occur to me that it was something one could make a living at. After graduating art school I worked in a magazine art department, where I was on the hiring end of illustration jobs. It was then that I realized what I really wanted to do.

What's your most embarrassing childhood memory?
Being a total klutz in elementary school gym class, and therefore usually being last to be picked for teams.

What's your favorite childhood memory?
There are so many. The anticipation of a game of flashlight tag on a hot summer night with the kids on the street where I grew up. Driving out to see my grandparents at the beach in the summertime, where my grandfather taught us how to fish

with a dropline off a dock. Being together with all of my cousins at the beach.

How did you celebrate publishing your first book?
This is terrible to say, but I can't remember! We probably went out to dinner. Our kids were really young then, so maybe I took a nap!

Where do you work on your illustrations?
I have a studio at home. (I love calling it a "studio"!) In reality it's a small room crammed full of two drawing tables (one for standing and one for sitting), my computer, bookshelves and sketches, art, and random inspiring stuff taped to the walls. Usually there's a cat (or two) and the dog hanging around as well. I'm a big fan of cozy clutter.

Where do you find inspiration for your illustrations?
My animals, dreams, other artists, Mother Nature, history, a funny phrase . . . in other words, everywhere.

Where do you go for peace and quiet?
It could be a hike in the woods, sitting on the beach, or walking around New York City. I think peace and quiet is a state of mind.

What makes you laugh out loud?
The interaction between our two cats and one dog. They're always getting themselves into funny situations.

What's your favorite song?
Anything that makes me want to sing out loud (enough to embarrass myself) and get up and dance.

Who is your favorite fictional character?
Laura from the Little House books.

What are you most afraid of?
Car crashes, cancer, climate change. Though I do try not to worry.

What's your favorite TV show or movie?
Lately I've been obsessed with *Downton Abbey*.

If you were stranded on a desert island, who would you want for company?
Someone with a sense of humor, and hope. (And a stack of books to pass the time.)

What's the best advice you have ever received about illustrating?
Observe. Keep drawing. Practice, practice, practice! Also, take joy in the process of creating.

What do you want readers to remember about your books?
I hope they bring a sense of warmth and comfort.

What would you do if you ever stopped illustrating?
Probably something to do with travel and languages. I'm a map illustrator in addition to my children's book work, so I love imagining what different places around the world are like. I'm also always trying to improve my French and Spanish, and I would love to learn Chinese one day. Foreign languages have always seemed like keys to another world to me.

What do you like best about yourself?
I have a good sense of humor.

What do you consider to be your greatest accomplishment?
Being a mom and a working artist at the same time.

What do you wish you could do better?
Be a mom and a working artist at the same time. Seriously, it's hard to do it all, but worth it to keep trying.

What was your favorite thing about school?
Art class. And free reading time in the classroom, after assignments were done.

What was your least favorite thing about school?
Gym.

If you could travel anywhere in the world, where would you go and what would you do?
I'd be happy to travel anywhere, but I have a particular love for France. I'd enjoy the sights, the food, the people . . . everything.

Who is your favorite artist?
Too many to pick one! Some random favorites are Lisbeth Zwerger, Garth Williams, Roger Duvoisin, Etienne Delessert, Edward Gorey, Shaun Tan, David Small, Christine Davenier, Valeri Gorbachev, Ashley Wolff . . . I could go on and on.

What is your favorite medium to work in?
Pencils, pen & ink, and watercolor.

What were your hobbies as a kid? What are your hobbies now, aside from illustrating?
As a kid I read a lot, wrote and drew in my journals, and was obsessive about horses. I have less free time now, but I still love to read. Also, I spend a lot of time puttering around in the garden.

What challenges do you face in the artistic process, and how do you overcome them?
The biggest challenge is overcoming self-doubt about my work. Over the years I've just learned to talk myself through it and keep moving forward. I find it comforting to know that many other artists have the same struggle. I must be normal!

About the Author

VALERIE HOBBS lives in Santa Barbara with her husband, Jack, and near her two amazing grandsons. She writes about dogs because she wants one of her own, but her ferocious cat, Molly, won't allow it. Visit her on the Web at valeriehobbs.com.

About the Illustrator

JENNIFER THERMES lives in an old house with her husband and children, two cats, one dog, and countless mice. She is a graduate of Parsons School of Design. Visit her on the Web at jenniferthermes.com.